"I want to take you to an FBI safe house."

"Is this one of those protected witness programs? Where you give up your identity?" She shook her head, sending ripples through her black hair. "That's unacceptable."

"It's the only way to be sure you're safe."

"I can't pick up and leave. I have responsibilities."

Denial was one thing. This attitude was insanity. "We're dealing with a serial killer. Make no mistake, Cara. He'll come after you again."

Her forehead pinched together in a frown. "But there must be another way. I don't want to be at a safe house. I want my life back. I don't want to be alone...."

"You're not alone." Dash sat on the edge of the bed. His hand rested on her shoulder. "I'm here."

CASSIE MILES

PROTECTIVE CONFINEMENT

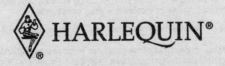

HARLEQUIN®

TORONTO • NEW YORK • LONDON
AMSTERDAM • PARIS • SYDNEY • HAMBURG
STOCKHOLM • ATHENS • TOKYO • MILAN • MADRID
PRAGUE • WARSAW • BUDAPEST • AUCKLAND

Thanks to my daughter, Kersten, for her help on all things anthropological. And, as always, to Rick.

ISBN-13: 978-0-373-88752-1
ISBN-10:   0-373-88752-3

PROTECTIVE CONFINEMENT

ABOUT THE AUTHOR

For Cassie Miles the best part about writing a story set in Eagle County near the Vail ski area is the ready-made excuse to head into the mountains for research. Though the winter snows are great for skiing, her favorite season is fall when the aspens turn gold.

The rest of the time Cassie lives in Denver where she takes urban hikes around Cheesman Park, reads a ton and critiques often.

Books by Cassie Miles

HARLEQUIN INTRIGUE

769—RESTLESS SPIRIT
787—PROTECTING THE INNOCENT
820—ROCKY MOUNTAIN MYSTERY*
826—ROCKY MOUNTAIN MANHUNT*
832—ROCKY MOUNTAIN MANEUVERS*
874—WARRIOR SPIRIT
904—UNDERCOVER COLORADO**
910—MURDER ON THE MOUNTAIN**
948—FOOTPRINTS IN THE SNOW
978—PROTECTIVE CONFINEMENT†

*Colorado Crime Consultants
**Rocky Mountain Safe House
†Safe House: Mesa Verde

CAST OF CHARACTERS

Cara Messinger—A 32-year-old, half Navajo archaeology professor who is the only surviving victim of a serial killer.

Dash Adams—After a privileged upbringing, he chose to become an FBI special agent. His current assignment is to investigate the serial murders and protect his witness.

The Judge—Legendary serial killer from the San Francisco area who is now active in Mesa Verde.

Russell Graff—An archaeology grad student who is obsessed with Cara, his former professor.

Flynn O'Conner—FBI special agent in charge of the Mesa Verde safe house.

Jonas Treadwell—A psychiatrist specializing in criminal psychology. He works with the FBI to profile the killer.

William Graff—The wealthy, powerful father of Russell Graff is determined to thwart the investigation.

George Petty—Archaeology professor supervising the dig site near Mesa Verde, where Russell worked.

Alexander Sterling—Renowned forensic anthropologist who unlocks the secrets of the bones.

Joanne Jones—Archaeology student having a dig-site romance with Russell Graff.

Yazzie—Cara's big, fat, yellow-striped tomcat.

Chapter One

Cara Messinger hated coming home to an empty house. Especially after dark.

At 11:22 on a Thursday night, she parked at the curb in her quiet neighborhood on the outskirts of Santa Fe and glanced toward her house. Two front windows stared back as if mocking her hesitation. Shadows from the windswept shrubs and piñon pines skittered across the white stucco walls like a thousand spiders gone wild.

She wasn't usually so nervous. Cara thought of herself as being responsible, strong and resourceful. A bit of an over-achiever. At age thirty-two, she'd been an archaeology professor for three years. She'd supervised digs and published academic papers. Other people respected her. Young women wanted to *be* her. Why was she crouched behind the wheel of her car, afraid to go into her own house?

It had to be the e-mails. For the past two months, she'd been receiving weird e-mails from someone who called himself *the Judge.* He was watching her, stalking her.

"Well, watch this," she muttered as she shoved open her car door.

The night brought a chill to the thin air of the high desert even though it was spring-time. She shivered as she gathered her brief-case and books from the back seat. When she slammed the car door, the sound echoed. From somewhere down the block, a dog howled.

Her keys jingled in her hand as she hurried up the sidewalk, and her sense of apprehension grew stronger. She was not alone in the night. Someone else was here. Something else. She felt a heavy jolt against her ankle and staggered backward. Her books fell on the concrete porch.

Two unblinking yellow eyes stared up at her. "Yazzie."

The big orange-striped tomcat yawned.

"Yazzie, you scared me to death."

The twenty-pound tom threaded his bulk between her arms and batted at a strand of her long black hair as she bent down to retrieve her books. His purr rumbled as loud as a motorboat.

"You really are a pest." She'd never intended to have a pet, but Yazzie had adopted her. When he'd been only a kitten and the name Yazzie—Navajo for "little one"—had still applied, he'd shown up on her doorstep and had claimed this territory as his own. She really shouldn't complain; the big orange tom was the closest to a relationship she'd had in months.

Inside the house, she flicked the switch by the door. A soft overhead light shone on her earth-tone sofa, chairs and coffee table. Being home usually soothed her; this place was her sanctuary. Instead, her tension deepened—a possible result of the two cups of espresso she'd had with her students to celebrate her last evening lecture of the semester. This academic year was almost over. She should have been relieved.

Her gaze scanned the shelves by the door that held an array of native pottery, artifacts and woven baskets she'd acquired while working at various archaeological sites throughout the Southwest. Color from the woven Navajo rug on the hardwood floor brightened the room. Nothing seemed out of place.

Yazzie had picked up on her mood. Instead of dashing to his food dish in the kitchen and yowling until she fed him, he leaped onto the center of the coffee table. His back arched, he bared his sharp teeth and hissed.

A shudder went through her. Cats were good at sensing danger. "What is it, Yaz?"

He hissed again. Then he bolted toward her and out the door into the night.

For a moment, she considered following the cat. Racing back to her car. And then what? Sleep in the car? Rent a motel room? Ridiculous. There was nothing to be afraid of.

Firmly, she closed the door and crossed behind the sofa to the dining area where her laptop sat on the table. She dropped her books on the table, peeled off her wool jacket and logged on. *Might as well get this over with.*

Immediately, the threat appeared on her computer screen. She had an e-mail from "Judge." The message line said: Final. Possibly, a reference to final exams or final papers. The way she figured, her stalker had to be a student. A computer expert might be able to track him down, but Cara hadn't wanted to report the e-mails. She took enough grief for being the youngest person in the department. Young and female. And half-Navajo.

Angrily, she ignored the Judge and opened a message from the Navajo tribal council reminding her of the meeting next week at Window Rock. No problem. The meeting was already on her calendar.

The next e-mail came from her half sister who was getting married next month in Denver in an epic production worthy of Hollywood. Cara had been recruited as a bridesmaid—a position she wasn't thrilled about. For one thing, she was the oldest and ought to be getting married first. Also, Cara's father was Navajo while her three half sisters were the offspring of her mother's second husband, a blond, blue-eyed doctor. They looked just like him. Though they didn't consciously treat her like an outsider, she didn't fit into the family unit. With her long black hair amid all that blondness, she felt like a crow in a flock of canaries.

The only physical trait Cara had inherited from her mom was her pewter-gray eyes.

In the e-mail, her half sister reminded Cara about a final fitting for her coral-colored bridesmaid dress. Gritting her teeth, Cara responded that she was looking forward to those peachy ruffles and bows.

Then she opened the message from the

Judge. It started innocently enough. Good evening, Cara. Congratulations on finishing the semester.

This seemingly innocent comment quickly turned sinister.

You're very pretty tonight, the e-mail continued. Red is your color. Blood-red.

She glanced down at the dark crimson blouse she wore with a long khaki skirt. He'd been watching her tonight.

You really shouldn't drink coffee so late, Cara. You'll have the devil's own time falling asleep. Before you close your eyes, you might read the Nora Roberts book on your bedside table.

He knew what was on her bedside table. Damn it. He must have been here at her house, peeking through the windows. Until now, his comments had been limited to the campus and her car. He was coming too close for comfort.

He always signed off with "catch you later." Tonight, the difference was subtle but scary. Catch you soon.

She heard a creaking of floorboards and looked up. A tall young man stood in the hallway that led to her bedroom.

A scream caught in her throat. Her blood

turned to ice water. She knew this man. His name was Russell Graff. When he was in her class, she was aware that he might have a bit of a crush on her. But nothing like this. Nothing crazy. Struggling for control, she asked, "What are you doing here, Russell?"

"I came to see you, Cara."

He looked down at his sneakers. His thick brown curls fell across his forehead. Though he was the aggressor, his attitude was sheepish—almost as if he were embarrassed.

Hoping to assert her authority, Cara stood. She was the professor. She gave the orders. "You have to leave."

"I want you to come with me." His deep voice was almost inaudible. "There's something I want to show you."

If she remembered correctly, Russell was enrolled in a graduate program and working at a dig site near Mesa Verde. Maybe he'd uncovered an important artifact. But that didn't explain or excuse his presence here. *He'd broken into her house.* "How did you get in here?"

"I thought you'd leave the door open for me."

Why would he think that? They had no relationship.

"I had to break a window. Sorry." His lower lip trembled. "Come quietly, Cara. Don't make me hurt you."

His shyness was more frightening than if he'd been raging and snarling. He was holding back, restrained by a thin leash that might snap at any moment.

She had to get away from him. Slowly and carefully, she circled the dining table and picked up her car keys. If she kept her distance, she might make it to the front door. And then to her car.

While she moved, she kept talking. "You were always a good student, Russell. I remember that paper you did comparing the Mayan culture to the Anasazi."

Her thigh brushed against the sofa. The bulky piece of furniture stood between them. She continued, "Now you're working at the dig with Dr. Petty. I was hoping to join that site later this summer."

He looked up. His dark eyes were cold and flat. "The time for judgment is here."

The Judge. Just like in his e-mails. "Listen to me, Russell. You don't—"

He sprang into action, charging across the room toward her.

Just as quickly, she made a frantic run for

the door. He shoved aside the coffee table, caught hold of her wrist and yanked her toward him. "You're coming with me."

His grip tightened. Viselike, he squeezed. Pain shot up her forearm. He was skinny but strong. No way could she win in a physical struggle. "Russell, please. Tell me what you want. I'll cooperate."

His eyes blazed. "You're mine now, Cara."

When he pulled his hand from his jacket pocket, she saw a flash of silver. A knife?

In a frantic effort, she threw all her weight toward the door, wrenching free of his hold and stumbling to her hands and knees. She scrambled to her feet and ran.

At the door, he caught up to her and pushed hard against her shoulder. She crashed into the shelves of Native American artwork. Pottery, vases and kachinas shattered as they hit the hardwood floor.

She darted away from him. He cut off her escape, backing her into a corner. She stared in shock as he came closer. Russell Graff, an A student. A young man from a good family. He brandished the silver object in his hand.

"I'm sorry," he whispered.

She felt the metal prongs in her side, then the shock. A stun gun. Her body convulsed.

She felt as if her heart would explode. Her muscles twitched, tied into knots. Her legs weakened and she fell to the floor.

Fighting her way through excruciating pain, she forced her hand to clutch the arm of a chair. Every muscle in her body screamed as she clawed her way upright. Trembling in horrible spasms, she faced her attacker.

When he reached toward her, she made a feeble slap at his hand. He gave her a sad smile. "I didn't want to hurt you."

"B-bastard."

He plunged a hypodermic needle into her arm. Unable to fight him, unable to escape, she felt herself sinking into a dark, bottomless canyon.

CLUTCHING A FOAM CUP of caffeinated sludge, FBI Special Agent Dash Adams entered the home of Dr. Cara Messinger, archaeology professor. At a glance, he took in the obvious signs of a struggle. Furniture askew. Broken pottery on the floor. A Navajo rug crumpled against the sofa.

A plainclothes detective waved from the other side of the dining-room table. "Agent Adams, over here."

Dash couldn't remember if he'd met this detective before. During the past three days, he'd spoken to dozens of local investigators and issued a written memorandum outlining the profile of a serial killer who had been active in San Francisco three years ago. He'd been damned active, with seven documented kills in six months. Then the terror had ended. The killer had never been apprehended, never heard from again.

The FBI agents in the Violent Crime Apprehension Program had presumed he was dead or jailed for another crime. Now, Dash had reason to believe the ViCAP conclusion had been wrong. Five days ago, a New Mexico deputy had discovered the charred remains of a woman buried in a shallow grave, her wrists and ankles bound in a distinctive manner.

Dash had been sent to Santa Fe from the San Francisco bureau to head up this investigation. He wanted to believe that the arrangement of this corpse was nothing more than coincidence, but his gut told him differently. The Judge was active again.

Dash intended to succeed where ViCAP had failed. He wanted to close this case. Forever.

He shook hands with the Santa Fe detective. Though they were both wearing suits, the attitude in New Mexico was more relaxed. Knowing that, Dash hadn't bothered with a necktie.

The detective introduced himself. "Josef Meier."

"What have you got, Meier?"

"I think this is the guy you're looking for."

Though the detective's mouth pinched in a scowl, his eyes flickered with suppressed excitement that made him look too young for the grisly job of investigating a notorious serial murderer who restrained his victims for four days before finally killing them and burning their bodies beyond all recognition.

Meier's enthusiasm made Dash feel older than his thirty-four years. He was jaded, impatient. He dragged a hand through his close-cropped light brown hair and waited for Meier to continue.

"For one thing," Meier said, "the woman who went missing—Dr. Cara Messinger—fits the typical victim profile."

He held up a photograph of a young woman with long, straight black hair. In the picture, she wore baggy shorts and hiking boots. Her tanned legs were long and firm but not too muscular. Her shapeless khaki shirt didn't conceal her high, full breasts. A striking, attractive woman.

"Cara," Dash said. "Pretty name."

"Yes, sir."

Dash hoped he wasn't looking at a photograph that would be displayed at her memorial service. "How tall is she?"

"Five feet, seven inches. She's half-Navajo but wasn't raised on the reservation. Her eyes aren't brown."

"What color are they?"

"Hard to say. One witness said blue." He cocked his head and squinted into Dash's face. "Not a bright blue like yours."

Dash lifted a sardonic eyebrow. "Are you coming on to me, Detective?"

"No, sir." Meier straightened up. "Her driver's license says her eyes are gray."

Dash sipped his cold, murky coffee. Cara Messinger fit the profile, but that wasn't enough of a connection. There were a lot of dark-haired women who disappeared, and Dr. Messinger was more intelligent than the other victims of this killer. "She's a Ph.D., right?"

"An archaeology professor at the university. And she's only thirty-two."

A high achiever. Competitive. Dash understood that personality type. He'd graduated from Harvard Law with honors at twenty-three. After two years in private practice at a prestigious firm, he'd realized that he wanted to take a more aggressive approach to justice and had joined the FBI—a career path that his family despised. "What else have you got, Detective?"

Meier led the way through the small house to the rear bedroom. In spite of the guest bed, this room was clearly used as an office. Floor-to-ceiling bookshelves were crammed full. The oak desk was piled high with papers. The beautiful Dr. Messinger wasn't the tidiest woman on the planet. The lapse in perfection was endearing.

Meier pointed to the broken glass in a casement window. "I figure he got inside through here. He was waiting for her. That's part of your serial killer's modus operandi."

"Do you have proof that he was waiting for her?"

Meier shrugged. "I guess not."

Making assumptions was the downfall of too many investigations. Dash went to the casement window that opened with a crank—an open invitation to robbery. All an intruder had to do was break the glass, reach inside and unfasten the latch. He noticed the dust used by the CSI team to lift fingerprints.

"Prints?"

"Several," Meier said. "We're running them through the system. No identifications yet."

If this was the same guy, there wouldn't be traceable prints. He never left forensic evidence. Not a print. Not a hair. Not a fiber. "Tell me about your witnesses."

Meier referred to a notebook. "Dr. Messinger was reported missing today by a friend who was supposed to meet her for lunch."

"A boyfriend?" Often the individual who reported the crime was the perpetrator.

"Female. The friend got worried, came here, peeked through the window and called us." He flipped a page in his notebook. "The last time Dr. Messinger was seen was on Thursday night. She got home late after an evening lecture at the university."

Dash wasn't convinced that he was dealing with a serial killer. Not with so many other plausible explanations. Dr. Cara Messinger might have argued with a lover. Drugs could be involved. For all he knew, she'd had a psychological breakdown and decided to disappear all on her own.

A massive orange-striped cat stalked into the room, sprang onto the bed and glared at them.

Dash scowled back. "Who's this feline witness?"

"The neighbor said his name is Yazzie. The neighbor also reported that Dr. Messinger's car has been parked out front since Friday morning."

"Which backs up your theory that she was snatched on Thursday night." He sipped his coffee. "By a serial killer."

"It's more than a theory," Meier said heatedly.

The young detective wanted credit for making this connection, even though he was probably overreacting.

"Prove it to me," Dash said.

"There's one more piece of evidence."

As Dash and Meier returned to the front room, the cat followed, muttering cantankerous growls with every step.

Meier pointed to the laptop computer. "I just got it charged and booted up. Take a look."

Dash read the message line. *The Judge.*

A burst of adrenaline shot through his veins. If Meier was correct, Dr. Messinger had been abducted on Thursday night. The Judge always held his victims, toyed with them. He killed on the fourth day. Tomorrow. Sunday. "We need to move fast."

He picked up the photograph again and stared at the attractive black-haired woman. She must be going through hell right now.

Chapter Two

Her tongue was dry. The inside of her mouth tasted as if she'd been eating sand. A plastic water bottle stood on a chair beside the narrow bed, but Cara didn't dare drink from it.

Earlier, she'd figured out that the liquid in the water bottle was drugged, probably with a hallucinogen. Every time she'd taken a sip, her wits had gone numb. She'd become dizzy and docile, nearly unconscious. Then came the nightmares. Terrible apparitions of kachina demons. Snake dancers. And spiders, hundreds of spiders crawling over her flesh. Then came the drumming—a thunderous, intense, throbbing beat that had resonated in every cell of her body.

She shook her head to erase the horror of her dreams. *Focus, Cara.* Her imagination was nowhere near as bad as her reality. She was a captive with wrists and ankles bound. How long had it been? How many days and nights had she been locked inside this small, square room? She didn't know. Her memory floated in a dank miasma. A blur.

After the stun gun, he hadn't hurt her further. Russell had used a soft cotton rope that didn't dig into her skin, but the restraint was still painful. Her muscles ached. She needed to move, wanted to run.

Through the single, uncurtained window, she saw pinpricks of stars. The glimmer was mesmerizing. As she watched, the stars seemed to streak toward her, closer and closer. They became spears, aimed at her head.

With a frightened gasp, she turned away. Even the stars were against her. No one could help her.

Frustrated, she struggled against the rope that tied her hands in front of her. This couldn't be happening. But it was. She was here. A prisoner. And she had to escape.

Before she could think or reason, Cara needed to move. She sat up on the bed. Opened her eyes. Waited for the room to stop spinning.

She lifted the water bottle. God, she was thirsty. But she didn't drink. Carefully, she dribbled out a portion of liquid behind the bed, out of sight. It was important for Russell to think she was still drugged.

Now came the hard part: standing up. Her feet touched the worn, filthy carpet on the floor. Concentrating on balance, she stood. Her cramped muscles screamed. Her backbone felt as if she'd been twisted in a knot. *Ignore the pain.* She could do this. In baby steps, she inched toward the wooden table where Russell had laid out several items, including a knife.

She clutched the leather-covered haft of the knife in her stiff fingers. Every movement was clumsy. *Be strong. Concentrate.* She manipulated the knife until she was able to saw at the cord binding her wrists. The edge of the blade was dull. This would be a slow process, but it was her only chance.

There were other things on the table— ceremonial objects. A bowl of corn maize. A ceremonial pipe. Eagle feathers. A bundle of sage tied with twine. These things were used in a number of kachina dances and rituals, and she was disgusted that Russell had perverted Native American culture—her culture—for his own twisted purposes. Three votive candles cast flickering light on the dirty, unadorned walls.

She continued to work with the dull blade. Why had he left the knife?

Every time Russell had entered the room, he told her that she was being tested. She had to prove herself worthy. He was judging her. If she failed, she would die.

The knife slipped. The pointed tip slashed through her dark crimson blouse and pierced the flesh of her forearm. She cried out.

Oh no, what if he heard her? Standing very still, she listened for the sound of his footsteps outside the locked door. She heard nothing. No reaction to her outcry.

Russell might be sleeping. He might have left.

But he'd be back. She knew he'd be back. A wave of dread washed over her. He'd been in and out several times, bringing food and the drugged water. He had carried her, still bound, into the bathroom and insisted that she wash herself. He wanted her to be clean.

Though she couldn't remember, she thought she'd been bathed. Once, she'd awakened to find Russell brushing her hair and crooning. She had to get away from him.

Adjusting her grip on the haft, she dragged the dull blade across the rope. The cut on her arm dripped blood, hot as lava flowing down to her elbow. If she could slice through one strand of these complicated knots, she could work her way free.

Frustrated with her slow progress, she yanked. The bonds on her wrists tightened, cutting off circulation. But the rope was almost severed. With a final stroke, it tore apart.

Now she could work the knots loose. She replaced the knife on the table. Using her teeth, she tore at the knots.

Then she heard drumming from the outer room. The timbre and cadence reminded her of the Navajo powwows on the reservation. The drumming always came before Russell entered the room.

She couldn't allow him to see that she'd cut the rope. Moving as quickly as she could, Cara returned to the narrow bed and closed her eyes, pretending to sleep.

From outside the door, the drumming stopped. She heard voices raised in a heated conversation. Someone else was here. It wasn't the first time she'd heard another person. Another man. But she hadn't seen anyone but Russell.

She heard the snick of the key in the lock and curled into a ball. Her black hair fell across her face. She peeked through her nearly closed eyelids, watching Russell stride into the room. He was bare-chested.

He stood over her. "Cara, are you awake?"

She didn't respond. Through slitted eyes, she watched as he lifted the water bottle. "No more of this for you," he said. "I want you alert."

Why? What was he going to do to her?

He sat beside her on the bed. Roughly, he yanked her against his chest. Her cheek rested against his damp flesh. He smelled like sweat. She twisted her arms to hide the cut rope and the blood on her arm.

Cradling her head against his arm, he stroked her hair off her forehead. "You're mine, Cara. You belong to me."

His voice was as gentle as an adoring lover, and she fought the bitterness that curdled in her stomach.

He caressed her shoulders. At her elbow, his hand strayed to her breast and he cupped her. It took an effort not to lash out. Not to complain. She had to make him think she was unconscious and pray that he wouldn't notice the cut strand of rope.

"You're mine," he whispered. "You're different from the others."

Others? Had there been other women?

"You'll see it my way," he said. "You'll realize that we're meant to be together. It won't be much longer. Only a few hours until dawn."

And then what?

Abruptly, he shoved her out of his arms. She fell back on the bed, forcing herself not to move, not to speak.

He left the room, and she heard the key in the lock.

She had to escape before sunrise.

DASH UNHOLSTERED HIS PISTOL and adjusted his Kevlar vest. A night breeze rushed against his face but the wind did nothing to cool his agitation. He was on the verge of apprehending the Judge.

He'd selected a team from the Santa Fe FBI and the local police, including Detective Meier, who had been alert enough to notice the e-mail from the Judge on Cara's computer.

Tracking the e-mail had led through several blinds but finally produced results. The messages had originated with Russell Graff, age twenty-four, a former student of Dr. Cara Messinger. Russell had lived in San Francisco until three years ago when he'd left for college in Santa Fe. His departure coincided with the time when the Judge serial killings ceased.

As soon as Dash had a name, gathering information was relatively simple. A phone call told him that Russell Graff had left the site of the archaeology dig in southern Colorado where he had been working. He'd used a credit card to rent an adobe-style bungalow at the Broken Bow Resort on the outskirts of Santa Fe.

At one time, this seedy collection of run-down huts might have merited "resort" status. Not anymore. A poorly maintained dirt pathway wandered around an unfilled swimming pool. Twelve broken-down bungalows formed an outer circle. Even in the dark, Dash could see myriad cracks in the stucco walls. The wooden doors were scarred and scratched. Windows were filthy. Only two other renters had to be evacuated.

Dash and his team surrounded Bungalow

Seven, rented by Russell Graff, aka the Judge. His car wasn't here, but a light shone through the crack in the curtains.

Dash signaled to the two men with the battering ram. Silently, they moved into place.

With a glance toward Meier, Dash whispered a reminder. "We need to take him alive."

The detective nodded. "There are other murders to solve."

Murder? Dash hoped not. He hoped they'd be in time to rescue Dr. Cara Messinger.

He gave a nod to the two men with the ram. They drew back and let go. The door crashed open.

Dash raced through. "FBI. Freeze."

His warning echoed through empty space. He ran through the front room and kitchenette, charged into the bedroom and bathroom. His men swarmed into the place, searching for a man who wasn't here.

Dash should have known that the capture wouldn't be so easy. For years, this serial killer had eluded the FBI's top profilers and forensic ViCAP experts.

Was Russell Graff the Judge? Or had they been wrong? Had the trace on his e-mail been a mistake?

Dash stood in the bedroom of the bungalow and faced the mirror. His gun hung loosely at his side. With his other hand, he pointed to the mirror.

"That's one hell of a clue," Dash said.

The reflective surface was almost completely covered with photographs of Cara and scribbling that would provide hours of analysis for the profilers.

Dash knew they were on the right trail, and they didn't have much time. It was after midnight on Saturday. Technically, it was Sunday—the fourth day that Cara Messinger had been missing.

The Judge always killed on the fourth day.

RUSSELL'S HOARSE CRY ECHOED through the night, piercing her eardrums. "You're mine, Cara."

She ducked behind a juniper and wished herself invisible. The aftereffects of the drugs he'd been feeding her had distorted her perceptions while, at the same time, sharpening her senses. The fresh scent of juniper and earth mingled with the rank smell of her own fear. Which way should she run? Where should she go? She couldn't think, couldn't decide.

After she'd worked free from the ropes and climbed through the window, she'd faced a vast, surreal vista of low sage, cactus and trees. Faraway porch lights glimmered from other small houses. There was a two-lane road. No traffic. In the distance, she'd spied an intersection and a lit gas station attached to another building. A diner? A convenience store? *Go there. They might be open all night.*

Her instincts had kicked in then, warning her not to make a beeline toward the neon signs. She'd be too easy to track, too easy to find.

Instead, she'd run in the opposite direction. Her long khaki skirt tangled around her legs. The hard, rock-strewn soil tore at her bare feet.

The waning moon hung low in the west. She circled toward the gas station. Then she heard him. He screamed like a wild predator. An animal. "You're mine."

Terror raced through her. Hiding behind the juniper, she heard gunshots. Not just one. He fired a whole clip. As she huddled in the dark, she imagined the bullets tearing through her body, leaving ragged, bleeding tatters in her flesh. A hallucination. She hadn't been hit. But she felt the wounds; they were as real as the cut on her arm.

She remained utterly still, a rabbit hiding from a hawk, and she prayed. Someone would hear his rampage. Someone would call the police.

Though her heart raced, a heavy pall of exhaustion weighted her down. She sank to her knees. Peering through the juniper branches, she watched as he loped toward the gas station, full of vigor, terrifying in his purpose.

Abruptly, he stopped. His neck craned, and he stared in her direction. She felt his gaze. Her skin prickled. *Don't move. Don't let him see you.*

He threw back his head and yelled, "Cara!"

Her name ricocheted off the landscape. The sound was terrible and insane. Then came a low, threatening whisper that cut through the night air. "I'll never stop until I have you. Never."

He turned back toward the house and went inside.

Now. She should move now.

Gathering her strength, she stumbled toward another tree. Though she hadn't planned it this way, she was close to the intersecting road. If a car came this way, she might flag them down. But her strength was gone. She could barely put one foot in front of the other.

An explosion erupted behind her. The small house where she'd been held captive burst into flames. She saw Russell's car driving away. Toward this road. She had to get away from the road.

Frantically, she backtracked. Her breath came in shallow, rapid gasps.

Which way should she run? Toward the gas station or farther into the sheltering darkness? Her toe stubbed painfully against sandstone. She fell facedown. *Get up, Cara. You have to run, have to escape.* But the rich smell of the earth comforted her.

Mother Earth would protect her. She was part Navajo. They were *dineh,* people of the earth.

She closed her eyes. Consciousness faded.

When her eyelids opened, she was aware that much time had passed. The moon had almost set. The edge of dawn lightened the skies. It was a new day, and she was looking up into a pair of the most intensely blue eyes she had ever seen.

"Are you Cara?" he asked.

She nodded. Instinctively, she knew she could trust this man. He wouldn't hurt her.

"I'm Dash Adams. I'm with the FBI and I'm here to help you," he said. "It looks like your feet are hurt. May I help you stand up?"

"Yes." She appreciated his courtesy in asking rather than grabbing her.

She struggled upright. Her muscles were weak, and the world was spinning. No way would she be able to walk. Gently and carefully, he scooped her off the ground and held her. "You're going to be all right, Cara."

She believed him. Her cheek rested against his windbreaker. Her head tilted back, and she studied his face. His forehead was smudged with grime. Dark stubble outlined a strong jaw. His deep-set blue eyes shone with a determined light.

He'd said his name was Dash, and he was with the FBI. What was the FBI doing here? She knew there was a simple answer, but her brain wasn't working properly. Only one coherent train of thought presented itself. "I want to go home."

He said nothing. Didn't he hear her? She repeated, "I want to go home now."

"It's not safe. He knows where you live."

"Russell Graff." Her blissful moment of forgetfulness was over. A series of nightmare images clicked through her mind. The stun gun. The Judge. The ropes. Drugs. Spiders. She was lucky to still be alive. "You didn't catch him."

"No."

She jostled in his arms. "He said I belonged to him. He would never stop until he had me again."

He gazed down at her. The expressive light from his eyes communicated with her at a deep, primitive level. He was a warrior, her protector. "I won't let that happen."

She became aware of many other people. There were flashing lights from police cars and an ambulance. Firefighters controlled the flames from the small house where she'd been held captive. The stucco walls had crumbled—destroyed by the fire. Soon the embers would turn to ash and blow away on the arid winds.

More than anything, she wanted to forget that this had ever happened, to erase the pain and the humiliation of her abduction.

Suddenly, she was surrounded. Dozens of voices asked questions, while other hands reached for her.

She fastened her arms tightly around Dash's neck and looked up at him. "Don't leave me."

"I won't let you out of my sight."

At the ambulance, Dash handed her over

to the paramedics, who immediately checked her vital signs. He stayed close. When he'd promised to keep an eye on her, he'd been telling the truth. He needed Cara. She was his only witness.

When Russell Graff, aka the Judge, was finally apprehended, it would be Cara's eyewitness testimony that would ensure the sick bastard got what he deserved.

Dash watched as the paramedics draped a blanket over her shoulders and treated her wounds. A knife slash on her arm. Bruising at her wrists and ankles. Her knees and the bottoms of her feet showed several small lacerations.

One of the paramedics informed him that her injuries appeared to be mostly superficial, but she'd been drugged. They needed to take her to the hospital for tests. He arranged to ride along with them.

When he approached Cara, he could see that she was more alert, more in control of herself. The glaring lights from the ambulance reflected on her high cheekbones. Her gray eyes, surrounded by thick black lashes, snapped with fierce intelligence.

She didn't precisely fit the profile for the Judge's victims. Though Cara had the long, dark hair and slender build that the Judge preferred, she was taller than the others at five feet, seven inches. The other women had been small, almost doll-like. Also, Cara was older, in her thirties. And she was a professor, obviously intelligent. Harder to control.

In a firm voice, she announced, "I'm not going to the hospital."

"They need to run tests," Dash said. "You were drugged."

"I want to go home." She lifted her chin and confronted him directly. "If I can take a shower and change clothes, I'll be fine."

She was deep in denial. Not surprising, considering what she'd been through. Though her clothing was tattered and long black hair hung in tangles, she managed to project an attitude of control. She was one hell of a strong woman.

"You need to be checked out in the hospital," Dash said firmly. "Then I'll take you home."

Reluctantly, she conceded. "All right. But you promise I can go home?"

"Absolutely." It was better to humor her right now. He was damn sure that she wouldn't like his plans for her immediate future.

Chapter Three

In the hospital emergency care unit, Cara was poked and prodded and examined from head to toe. She'd been glad to shed her filthy clothing, but the thin cotton hospital gown offered little protection from the bone-deep chill inside her. With a blanket across her lap and another around her shoulders, she sat on a hard bed inside a curtained space. Dash stood beside her.

She looked up at him. "What day is it?"

"Sunday morning."

Russell had taken her captive on Thursday night. He'd held her all day Friday and Saturday. She counted on her fingers. "Four days."

"I need to ask you a few questions, Cara."

Her mind struggled toward coherency, and she remembered that he was with the FBI. In his black leather jacket and blue jeans, he didn't look like a Fed. "Are these official questions? Like a police report?"

"Later we'll do a recorded interview. And I'll want you to write a narrative while the details are still fresh in your mind."

She wasn't looking forward to putting her memories down on paper, but she'd do anything to help. Russell had to be stopped. "Why is the FBI involved?"

"The Judge is our investigation."

The Judge? She recognized the name from Russell's e-mails. But Dash made him sound like a known entity. "Why?"

When he glanced toward her, Dash seemed to be taking inventory, assessing her emotional state.

Defiantly, she stared back at him. She'd been through hell, but she'd survived. Her plan was to put these four days behind her and as quickly as possible, move on with her life. "Tell me the truth. Why does the FBI care about Russell Graff?"

"You're not his first victim."

There were others. Other women who had been abducted. "Are they…"

"Dead."

She swallowed hard. Inside her head, she

heard the echo of shamanic drumming. A shiver went through her. She could still feel his hands sliding over her body, could see his face contorted with rage. *He's not here. You're safe. You have to control yourself.*

Her mind was strong. She wouldn't allow herself to be ruled by trauma. "Are you telling me that Russell Graff is a serial killer?"

"If I say too much, I might prejudice your thinking. Right now, I want you to remember anything that might give me a clue to Russell's whereabouts. Did he mention other locations?"

"I don't think so."

"Take your time," he urged. "What did he talk about?"

She pulled the blanket more tightly around her shoulders. "If he's a serial killer, why haven't I read about him in the newspaper?"

"Did he talk about the dig where he's been working?"

"No."

"Did he mention any names?"

"No." Her memory cracked open. A torrent of confusion and fear flooded through her. She'd heard another voice. "Someone else was in the house with him."

His blue-eyed gaze sharpened. "Tell me more."

"I heard them arguing. It was another man."

"Did you see him?"

"No."

"Would you recognize his voice if you heard it again?"

"I doubt it. They were outside the door, and I was drugged. Everything is foggy."

"But you're certain you heard another voice?"

"Positively certain. Is that important?"

"Yes."

Her ordeal was not yet over. In a way, it had just begun. Cara knew now that she'd be forced to relive the events of her abduction again and again. To her, that sounded like hell. She'd always been a private person, staying below the radar and concentrating on her research and her classes. Her personal life was nobody else's business.

And she wasn't sure how helpful her memories would be to an investigation. She'd been drugged. How could she sort reality from hallucination? "What happens next?" she asked.

"Assuming the doctors say you're all right, you'll be released to my custody."

"Custody?" The word put her on edge. "I'm not a suspect, am I?"

"A witness. You're a very important witness."

"Why so important?"

"Because you're alive," he said. "And I intend to keep it that way."

"That sounds like a fine idea to me."

When he grinned, Dash looked like a different person. A guy who might enjoy having a good laugh now and then. His vocabulary and his attitude suggested that he was fairly well-educated. Not that it mattered. She needed to be careful to avoid thinking of him as a friend. Dash Adams was an FBI agent. Her only value to him was as a live witness.

"When can I go home?" she asked.

He cleared his throat. "I should prepare you for what we're going to find at your house. When you were reported missing, your home became a crime scene."

"What does that mean?"

"It's a mess," he said. "Forensic technicians have been going through your belongings, dusting for fingerprints, looking for trace evidence."

"Yazzie," she remembered. "My cat. A big orange tom. Is he all right?"

"Your neighbor is taking care of him."

Yazzie must be furious about all the strangers coming and going at her house, invading his territory. "Yazzie knew Russell was in my house when I got home. He hissed and snarled and ran out the door. That's what I should have done."

"We figured Russell was already inside," he said. "He was waiting for you."

What had he been doing? How had Russell passed the time while waiting to destroy her life? Revulsion tightened her gut as she imagined him touching her things, lying on her bed, using her toilet. In her mind, she could see him standing at her open closet door, surveying the clothing he'd taken such delight in describing in his e-mails. "When do you think you'll catch him?"

"I don't know."

That wasn't the answer she wanted to hear. Dash appeared to be a strong, competent person. He ought to be able to give her some idea of when Russell would be apprehended. "Two days? A week?"

"I'll do everything in my power to take him into custody."

That wasn't a direct answer. "Everything

in your power, huh? Are you good at what you do?"

His gaze was steady and confident as he replied, "I'm the best."

THOUGH THE DOCTORS SUGGESTED that Cara be hospitalized for observation, her physical condition checked out. She'd managed to eat something solid and had been drinking plenty of water. Apart from the occasional blur of hallucination at the edge of her peripheral vision, she was okay and demanded to be taken home.

Wearing hospital scrubs and a robe, she slipped into Dash's rental car. She had no idea how his car had gotten to the hospital since he'd ridden with her in the ambulance. He seemed to be able to make things happen with a few words into his ever-present cell phone, and she had no doubt that it was Dash giving the final nod that caused the doctors to release her.

He pulled up to the curb outside her house and parked behind her car. Though he'd warned her that she might not like what she found at home, Cara shuddered at the sight of yellow crime-scene tape tangled in her shrubs. *Oh, God, this is embarrassing.* All her neighbors would know what had happened to her. She'd be the center of gossip and speculation.

Dash circled the car and opened the door for her. She was determined to walk into her house without leaning on him. If she moved slowly, it wasn't too painful.

At the porch, Dash tore off the seal and used a key to open her front door. Inside, she faced the chaos of broken pottery and kachinas—the aftermath of her struggle. Her gaze went from the shelves to the floor where her favorite possessions lay shattered.

Anger exploded in a red burst behind her eyelids. "I want this to be over. Let's do the formal interview now. Then I can write out my narrative on my laptop."

"We've confiscated your computer."

"You can't do that." She glared at him. "I have a lot of information stored on that laptop. Papers that I'm working on. Research."

"We'll make sure we don't lose any of your files. Everything will be backed up."

"I need my computer." Though it was the end of the semester, there was still a lot going on at the university. "I have my students' grades on spreadsheets."

"Your laptop is evidence. We used it to

trace e-mails from the Judge. That's how we knew about Russell Graff."

"You could trace those e-mails?" She felt incredibly foolish. If she'd reported the threats right away, she would have known Russell's identity. The authorities would have been alerted. "I could have prevented this whole thing."

"Don't blame yourself. Even if you had known Russell's identity, you couldn't guess his intentions."

She picked her way carefully through the shards. Her meticulously arranged life was falling apart before her eyes.

"My mother," she said suddenly. "Does my mother know what happened?"

"I spoke to her yesterday," Dash said.

Oh, God! "I need to call her right now."

WHILE SHE WAS IN THE SHOWER, Dash filled in reports and made arrangements. A chopper would be waiting for them at the airport. All he had to do now was convince Cara to go along with his plans.

He turned off the ringer on her telephone. Even though he'd warned the other officers, agents and firemen to keep the abduction quiet, it was only a matter of time before the news leaked. The media would be all over Cara. She was an attractive woman—one who would play well on television.

When she emerged from the bedroom wearing jeans and a soft white tunic, she looked a hundred percent better. In her sneakers, she was even walking with more confidence. The gray of her eyes was less murky.

Her recovery would have been miraculous…if he believed it. Cara was putting up a damn good facade, pretending that she wasn't in the least traumatized. Later, he knew, she'd crash. Maybe not today or tomorrow. But soon.

She beamed a huge smile, but it wasn't for his benefit. The big orange tomcat had sauntered into the room.

"Yazzie." Cara squatted down to his level. "Come here, baby."

Whipping his tail, the cat bulldozed his way into her waiting arms and allowed himself to be lifted. When he glanced toward Dash, he bared his sharp teeth and hissed.

"Stop it," she chided the cat. "Dash is one of the good guys."

Yazzie hissed again.

"Fine with me," Dash muttered. Pets were

a pain in the rear. "I don't need to be friends with a furry Jabba the Hutt."

Defensively, she said, "He has a healthy appetite."

"Obviously."

She sat at the end of the dining table with the cat sprawled over her lap. "When I talked to my mother in Denver, I convinced her that everything was fine and she didn't need to come down here and take care of me."

"That must have taken some convincing." If he'd had a daughter who'd been held captive by a serial killer, he'd walk through fire to be with her. "Are you and your mother close?"

"Fairly close." An involuntary grimace tugged at the corner of her mouth. "She was married to my father for only five years. For most of that time, he wasn't around."

"She remarried."

She shot him a curious look. "How do you know that?"

"FBI," he reminded her. "We know everything."

"Well, yes. She remarried. My stepfather is a great guy. A doctor. And I have three half sisters. All blond."

Which made Cara the outsider. He was beginning to understand her need to prove herself. "How much did you tell your mother?"

"Not everything." She straightened her shoulders and said, "I'm ready to do that formal interview and written report. Let's get this over with."

"There's something we need to discuss first." There was no easy way to break this news. "Like I said before, you're an important witness, and you need to be protected. I want to take you to an FBI safe house."

"Is this one of those protected witness programs? Where you give up your identity?" She shook her head, sending ripples through her thick black hair. "That's unacceptable."

"It's the only way to be sure you're safe."

"I can't pick up and leave. I have responsibilities." She stroked Yazzie vigorously. "This is the end of the semester. Next week are final exams. I have a ton of papers to be graded."

Denial was one thing. This attitude was insanity. "We're dealing with a serial killer. Make no mistake, Cara. He'll come after you again."

Her forehead pinched in a frown. "Of course, I don't want to take risks, but there must be another way. I don't want to be at a safe house. I want my life back."

"He's a serial killer." Though Dash was trying to be sensitive, he grew impatient. "Trust me. I know what's best."

"What if you don't find him for weeks? I have places I need to be. There's a Navajo tribal council meeting this Thursday that I can't miss. My half sister is getting married and I need to go up to Denver for a fitting on my bridesmaid dress."

"Neither of which is important compared to your personal safety."

"There must be some other way. I could hire a bodyguard."

Dash wasn't about to leave her protection to some half-baked rent-a-cop. He stood and picked up his car keys. "Come with me, Cara. There's something you need to see."

IT WAS A SHORT DRIVE to the Broken Bow Resort. In the morning light, the place looked even more seedy and dilapidated than the night before when Dash and his men had charged into an empty bungalow.

"Why are we here?" she asked.

"Russell rented one of these bungalows.

We thought he was holding you here." He shoved open the car door. "Come with me."

Her gait was halting, and he could see that she was half-exhausted though she wouldn't admit her weakness to the paramedics or him. Or even to her mother.

As they approached, he nodded toward a motor home. Inside were a couple of agents who were keeping an eye on the place in case Russell returned.

Last night, they'd gone through this door with a battering ram. Though it appeared to be closed, the lock didn't work. Dash pushed it open and walked into the dingy little room. "Russell isn't going to give up easily. He wants you, Cara."

"I know," she said quietly.

"He'll do anything to get his hands on you again. Anything."

In her eyes, he saw a healthy glimmer of fear; she was beginning to comprehend the danger that surrounded her.

In the bedroom, he directed her toward the mirror. "Take a look."

Taped to the mirror were fourteen snapshots of Cara in various settings. In the classroom. Walking across the campus. Laughing. Poring over a textbook. Each picture was carefully annotated with time and date. The center photo was inside a lipstick heart. Above it all was a neatly printed banner that read: Mine in Life. Mine in Death.

"He's obsessed with you," Dash said. "He won't give up until he has you."

She turned on her heel and walked out of the bedroom. Her hand covered her mouth, and he thought she might vomit. Her shoulders trembled. In a quiet voice, she said, "We need to return to my house. I'll need to pack a few things before I go with you."

"Smart decision."

"And I want to take Yazzie with me."

"Fine."

If it meant getting Cara to safety, he'd agree to a dozen furry orange beasts.

RUSSELL GRAFF WATCHED from the parking lot in front of the diner down the road from the Broken Bow Resort as Cara emerged from the bungalow. She'd found herself a protector, but it wouldn't do any good. She belonged to him. They were meant to be together.

He pulled his black cowboy hat lower on his forehead. As they drove past, he started his engine. It was a good thing that he was using a rental car. A good thing that he'd burned down the deserted house off Route 24, leaving no trace of evidence.

He merged into traffic and followed them. She was his property. Why didn't the bitch understand? It looked as if he needed to teach Professor Cara a lesson.

This time, he wouldn't be so gentle.

Chapter Four

If the circumstances had been different, Cara
would have been enthusiastic about riding in
a helicopter. The only other time she'd been up
in one of these things was a tourist excursion
on a family vacation in New York to view the
man-made wonder of the Manhattan skyline.

Out here—in the wide-open spaces of the
West—Mother Nature reigned supreme. An
ethereal blue sky surrounded the chopper as
they flew beyond the forested mountains
outside Santa Fe and headed northwest along
the route followed by the Rio Grande. A
varied topography spread below her. A wide
sandstone plain dotted with sagebrush and
juniper. A craggy, red cliffside. A broad, flat
mesa that cast shadows of deep purple
worthy of a Georgia O'Keefe painting.
"Beautiful," she murmured.

Even though she was wearing ear protection, she could hear the whir of the rotors and feel the vibration of the helicopter. Dash sat an arm's length away on the opposite side. His attention focused on a laptop computer balanced on his knees. Back to work? Apparently, today's events were business as usual for him.

For her, everything had changed. Her own laptop had been confiscated. Her cozy, academic life had been shattered like the pottery in her living room. Though she told herself that she really didn't care what other people thought, she wasn't looking forward to being singled out as the person who had been abducted by one of her former students. A serial killer. A stalker. A monster.

Residual fear pressed in around her, skirting the edge of her consciousness, threatening to emerge in a full-blown panic attack. She couldn't give in to these feelings.

Leaning back in her seat, she cradled Yazzie on her lap. He'd been screeching wildly inside his carrying case so she'd opted for using a leash fastened to a harness. As soon as she'd held him, he'd calmed down. His solid bulk comforted her. His fur was warm.

Her eyelids drooped. If she could sleep,

she might wake up feeling safe and secure. She might trick her mind into believing nothing was wrong. But as she drifted off, the nightmares approached. The beating of the shamanic drum. Footsteps in the hallway. Her skin prickled as she imagined spiders crawling across her arm.

She knew better than to be afraid of spiders. In many of the Navajo legends, Spider Woman was a powerful totem who taught the *dineh* how to weave their rugs and showed them the fabric of the Universe as she whispered eternal wisdom in their ears. Cara stilled her fears and listened. Spider Woman would help her and show her the path.

Her dreams shifted. In her sleep, she saw ancient patterns. Bright, happy colors. She imagined herself wrapped in a gauzy rainbow, stepping into a warm pool. Oh yes, this was good. Sighing with contentment, she soaked in healing waters.

Unbidden, Dash Adams entered her dream. The crystal-blue of his eyes mesmerized her. His broad chest was bare. His biceps flexed as he reached toward her. She welcomed his touch, his strong hands gliding over her body.

Sudden darkness descended. The image of Dash vanished. Her only light was through the single square window of her prison. Russell was coming for her. He'd never give up, never quit until he had her in his claws. He was the cougar, hunting alone and stalking his prey. Coming closer. His hot breath touched the back of her neck.

With a cry, she forced her eyelids to open.

Dash was touching her arm. "Are you all right?"

"Bad dream." She looked through the window. *Forget Russell. Don't let him get to you.* The sun was high in the sky. "What time is it?"

"A little after four o'clock. You've been asleep for over two hours."

The chopper swooped toward a vista of snow-capped peaks. When she leaned forward for a better view through the window, Yazzie scrambled around on her lap. The usually independent cat crawled up her torso, nuzzled against her throat and mewed pitifully. Though he'd allowed himself to be petted by the pilot, the cat had nothing but growls and hisses for Dash. Cara wondered if Yazzie was instinctively vying for her attention. Was the tomcat clever enough to sense that his mistress might be attracted to this cool, surprisingly sexy FBI agent?

She glanced toward him. Though his azure eyes were hidden behind dark sunglasses, she could tell that he was looking at her, scrutinizing her. The corner of his mouth cocked in a lazy grin, and she smiled back, perhaps a bit too broadly. A sudden warmth flushed through her. She remembered the first time she'd seen him—her rescuer. Her sensory memory was imprinted with the strength of his arms when he'd lifted her from the ground and carried her toward safety.

Because that was his job, she reminded herself. She'd be crazy to form any sort of attachment to him. As if to remind her to be cautious with her heart, Yazzie kneaded his claws on the shoulder of her shearling jacket.

She cleared her throat and pointed out the window. "What mountains are those?"

"San Juan Range in southern Colorado," Dash said. "We're going to the Four Corners region."

The juncture of Colorado, New Mexico, Arizona and Utah was near the famous cliff dwellings at Mesa Verde. She often took her classes on weekend field trips to that ancient city.

The archaeological site where Russell had been working was farther west, toward Chaco Canyon. Her gaze scanned the vast terrain as if she might possibly catch sight of him. A manhunt in this area would be terribly difficult. In these hills and valleys, Russell could hide out for a long time. He might never be caught.

If not, what would happen to her? She couldn't stay in protective custody forever. Even though she didn't have a boyfriend or a family of her own, Cara had a life. She had plans.

Dash touched her elbow and nodded toward the window. "That's the safe house."

The two-story white clapboard house with a red barn and an attached bunkhouse sat in the middle of a wide green valley bordered by forested foothills leading to the San Juan Range. Utterly isolated. There were no neighboring houses in sight. The surrounding landscape was buffalo grass, sage and the wildflowers of spring.

"Looks like a farmhouse," she said.

"It used to be."

When the chopper landed, she held tightly to the leash attached to Yazzie's harness. She didn't want the cat to run off and get lost in these unfamiliar surroundings.

The rotors stilled, and there was silence except for the blowing of the wind.

Holding Yazzie in her arms, she allowed Dash to help her down from the helicopter. The soles of her feet prickled inside her shoes from numerous cuts and scratches. Her muscles were sore and the wound on her arm hurt. But her mind was clearer. That was really the most important thing. As long as she could think, everything else would take care of itself.

When she placed Yazzie on the ground, the cat ducked down behind a clump of buffalo grass and refused to move even when she tugged on the leash. "Come on, Yaz. This is going to be your new home for a while."

"I could carry him," Dash offered.

"You could try," she said wryly. "But he doesn't seem to like you."

"We'll see."

He squatted down to the level of the cat and took off his sunglasses. They glared. It was a staring contest between man and feline. The first to look away would be the loser.

Dash lowered his voice. "You and me, cat. We both want the same thing. Cara's safety."

Yazzie hissed.

"You don't have to like me, but we damn well better get along. Truce?"

When Dash held his hand toward Yazzie, the cat leaned toward him, sniffed, then rubbed his head against the back of Dash's hand. Cara couldn't believe her stubborn cat had been so easily won over.

Then, Yazzie bared his teeth and nipped at Dash's knuckles, drawing blood.

Without flinching, Dash swept Yazzie off the ground and held him tightly against his shoulder. They were eyeball to eyeball.

After one final hiss, Yazzie settled against him and cast an arch look in Cara's direction.

"Nice job," she said. "I guess this officially makes you the alpha male."

"King of the cats."

He strode down a wide dirt pathway toward the split-rail fence that enclosed the house and barn, and she followed. Cara had thought an FBI safe house would be more clandestine. This charming white farmhouse with dark gray trim looked as clean and wholesome as fresh milk. Not that she'd know what milk straight from the cow tasted like. In spite of her Native American heritage, Cara had been raised in urban environments.

A tall, lanky cowboy sauntered down from the porch and approached them. His features were hard and chiseled; his hair and eyes were brown. He reminded her of a hard-edged wood sculpture as he eyed Yazzie.

"This is a first," he drawled. "A protected witness cat."

Dash introduced him. "Special Agent Flynn O'Conner. We worked together in San Francisco."

As she shook his callused hand, Cara saw a flash of sharp intellect in those brown eyes. "Are you familiar with the Judge?"

"He was my case. Before I took over the running of this safe house, I used to be with ViCAP."

Certainly, this was no coincidence. Dash had brought her to this particular safe house because Flynn O'Conner was an expert. Though Cara would rather forget what had happened to her, there was no escape.

WITH CARA AND JABBA THE CAT settled in one of the upstairs bedrooms, Dash went with Flynn into the kitchen, which appeared to be the largest room in this old ranch house. The windows over the sink faced the red painted barn with attached corral. Closer to the house were a couple of cottonwood trees, one of which had an old-fashioned wood swing hanging from the branches.

A family had once lived in this six-bedroom house, and this was a functional kitchen with a double oven and huge refrigerator. Pots and pans hung from a rack over a large butcher block, and there was a long table with benches where eight people could sit comfortably.

Flynn poured two mugs of coffee and brought them to the table. He looked tanned and relaxed—a hell of a lot healthier than the last time Dash had seen him in San Francisco. Toward the end of the Judge investigation, Flynn had been a wreck. Unable to sleep. Eating crap food. He'd refused to leave the office. Night and day, he'd pored over the case files. Special Agent Flynn O'Conner had blamed himself for the deaths of those seven women.

"You look fit," Dash said. "Colorado agrees with you."

"This is a plum assignment. Plenty of time to work out. Ride horses. We're not far from skiing at Telluride." His elbows rested on the tabletop as he lifted his coffee mug. "Sometimes it feels more like I'm running a bed-and-breakfast than an FBI safe house."

"How many people are staying here now?"

"Two protected witnesses, plus Cara and her cat. And I have a rotating staff of two newbie agents who do the cooking and cleaning. They file the reports and keep all the high-tech surveillance gear maintained."

"You never liked electronic equipment," Dash said.

"Computers will never be a substitute for instinct. Always go with your gut."

Dash had to wonder if his old friend was happy with this semiretirement. Back in San Francisco, Flynn had been one of ViCAP's best profilers; he'd pursued active investigations with a dogged intensity. "Tell me, Flynn. Do you miss it?"

"What?"

"The chase."

When Flynn shook his head, his hair fell across his forehead. The cut was a little too shaggy, too casual, too relaxed. "I'm not like you, Dash."

"What's that supposed to mean?"

"Supercompetitive. You're a risk-taker. An adrenaline junkie. You enjoy running headlong into danger, flying by the seat of your pants."

Not a flattering assessment. Dash would

have been ticked off if he hadn't heard this personality analysis at virtually every review session with his superiors. "It works for me."

"You get results." Flynn laced his fingers together on the tabletop. "But this time you're off and running in the wrong direction. This guy, Russell Graff, isn't the Judge."

Taking a moment to digest Flynn's plainspoken opinion, Dash sipped his coffee. "This brew isn't half-bad."

"One of the newbies is a coffee nut. We've even got an espresso machine."

"I like him already."

"How long are you planning to stay?" Flynn asked.

"Until the job is done. Cara is my best lead."

He'd promised that he'd stay with her and keep her safe. Not a bad assignment. She was easy on the eyes, and he liked her spirit.

In the chopper, he'd watched her as she'd slept fitfully. Even with her eyes closed, her face was expressive. Her lips were full but tense. The way she kept everything bottled up inside made her mysterious, made him want to know her better.

After another sip of the excellent coffee,

he turned toward Flynn. "You're sure this isn't the Judge?"

"Positive."

"The forensics and the autopsy on the first victim—the woman found in Santa Fe— were a fairly good match for the Judge's other kills."

"But there wasn't enough left of the ropes to know what kind of knots were used."

The forensic details hadn't been perfectly recorded, but there was enough evidence to make the connection. Dash enumerated the details. "The body was burned beyond recognition. The accelerant used was the same as the Judge. She was buried in a shallow grave."

"There was no note," Flynn said. "No grandstanding for the investigators. The Judge needs that attention, needs to feel like he's superior by outsmarting law enforcement."

"He did that with you."

"That's right." Though Flynn's voice stayed calm, his fingers tightened into fists. "When I was investigating him, he sent me personal letters. Taunts. He announced when he would kill again. He signed his letters with *aloha,* a word that means hello and goodbye."

"Russell Graff used the phrase *catch you later* in his e-mails to Cara."

"I'm telling you, it's not Russell Graff," Flynn said. "He's a twisted, sick son of a bitch who's probably obsessed with your pretty little professor. But he's not the Judge."

"He called himself *Judge* in the e-mails."

Flynn countered. "Why would he leave that evidence behind? Why not take her laptop? When he abducted Cara, he left fingerprints and trace evidence. The Judge never made a mistake like that."

"Do you really believe he's dead? In your gut. Do you believe it?"

Doubt flickered in Flynn's eyes. Though ViCAP had found a burned body in a hideout used by the Judge, the man identified had no prior connection to the crimes. "The proof is that the killing stopped."

"Maybe not. Maybe he just moved to New Mexico. Out here, in these wide-open spaces, we aren't as likely to find the bodies."

Stubbornly, Flynn repeated, "It's not Graff."

Though Dash respected Flynn's experience and his detailed knowledge of the serial murders in San Francisco, he wasn't about to dismiss the similarities between Russell Graff and the Judge. Evidence pointed to a resurrection; the Judge had risen from the ashes to kill again.

But was Russell the same killer who was active in San Francisco? Could those murders be pinned on him? Or had Russell taken on the Judge's legacy?

"Here's another theory," he said. "Russell Graff lived in San Francisco at the time when the Judge killings were making headlines. Russell was twenty-one. By most accounts, he was a quiet young man, a good student from a wealthy family."

"Not exactly the profile of a serial killer."

"Which profile is that?" Dash asked sarcastically. "Every time we investigate another one of these sick bastards, the profile changes."

"Tell me about Russell."

"Key character trait—he's obsessive," Dash said. "Let's assume he fixated on the Judge, identified with his seeming invulnerability and power."

"Could be."

It was an unfortunate fact that serial killers tended to have cult followings. Dash suspected that if they could check Russell's computer, they'd find that he was a frequent visitor to the dozens of Web sites devoted to the Judge's heinous exploits.

"Here's what I think," Dash said. "Russell Graff is a copycat killer."

RUSSELL LEANED AGAINST the locked door and listened to the whimpers of a young woman who looked like Cara. She wasn't as pretty. No other woman matched Cara's beauty. Certainly not this skinny little runt.

She kept sobbing. "Please. Please."

Her pathetic little cries disgusted him. He hadn't been careful in his selection, hadn't taken pictures of her, hadn't learned her habits.

It wasn't necessary to follow the rituals with her. He had already deemed her unworthy. The greatest value in her death would be to send a message, to show Cara that he would kill again and again. Until she came back to him, he would appease his rage with others. He would litter the earth with the burned remains of these sad, useless women.

He twisted the lock and entered her room, the ceremonial room. Moving fast, he went to the mattress where she lay. Her wrists and ankles were bound. She'd tossed aside the unzipped sleeping bag he'd used to cover her.

"Shut the hell up." He pointed to the drugged water bottle on the floor beside her mattress. "Drink your water."

"Please don't hurt me," she begged. "I'll do anything you want. Anything."

His fingers tangled in her long black hair. He yanked her head back. "I don't need your permission. You'll do anything I want because I own you."

Her fear and her struggling excited him, but it was too soon to take action. He would wait. Four days.

He left her and locked the door. Prowling, he circled the outer room in this deserted adobe house he'd used before. There was no furniture. Only his Navajo rug on the floor. And his drum.

He tucked the drum under his arm and tapped lightly. The sound resonated against the four blank walls of his lair as he played a ceremonial rhythm. Louder and louder. A low, guttural chant harmonized with the pulsing primitive beat.

Head thrown back, he wailed. There was no one here to tell him to be quiet. No one to frown and tell him that good boys didn't make noise. No one to punish him.

He was the punisher. He made the judgments.

His ears pricked up, listening for the sound of his mother's voice. Her criticism. *Mother, I'm sorry.*

He stopped playing.

The stillness was broken by weeping. Why couldn't he end it with this girl now? *Why do I have to wait?*

"Because that's the way it's done. Four days."

More than ever before, he needed to follow the rules. *I'll try to do this the right way.*

No wait. "I have a better idea."

He would use this girl. And others. They would send a message to Cara.

He was so close. He could feel Cara's thoughts all around him. She was his salvation.

Chapter Five

That evening, Cara stood at the window in her bedroom at the safe house. She'd just finished her formal interview and handwritten account of her abduction and captivity. It hadn't gone well. Practically every word she'd uttered had been followed by a disclaimer. "I *think* that's what happened. But I'm not *sure.*"

Agent Flynn O'Conner—who had conducted the interview—kept reassuring her that she was doing fine. But Cara knew she wasn't. Her memories were jumbled and rife with inaccuracies.

Had Russell touched her inappropriately? Yes, but she couldn't remember how many times or in what context. He'd seemed fascinated with her hair. Several times, he'd brushed her hair.

Had he beaten her? She remembered a slap. And horrible threats. He had used the knife, glided the flat of the blade along her cheekbone.

Over and over, he'd told her she was being judged and must prove herself worthy. But his actions and questions made no sense.

At the window, she pulled down the shade, shutting out the dusk. Downstairs, dinner was being served, but she'd told Flynn not to set a plate for her. She wasn't hungry. Plus, she didn't feel like meeting more strangers. Cara didn't want to explain herself, to define herself as the latest victim of a serial killer. Not that she had to. One of the rules of the safe house was not to discuss the reason you were there.

But Flynn knew. So did the other agents. And Dash.

She was mad at him. He should have been the one to interview her. Instead, he'd left the room, abandoned her—a clear reminder that she was only a witness in his eyes. Not a friend. Certainly not anything more. Any attraction she felt for him was imaginary; Dash wasn't the man who would step up and fill the empty spaces in her life.

Might as well face the obvious. She was alone. Except for Yazzie. He posed like a hefty orange-striped sphinx in the middle of the blue plaid comforter.

She stretched out on the bed beside him. "You and me, Yaz. You're my family."

He twitched his whiskers as if to remind her that he was, in fact, a cat. Not even the same species, he was a poor substitute for having a family of her own—a husband and kids, people who belonged together.

Rolling onto her back, she stared up at the white ceiling with the old-fashioned, tulip-shaped light fixture. Her gaze slid down the clean white walls and scanned the blue plaid curtains that matched the bedspread. She couldn't really complain about the accom-modations; this was a pleasant room with knotty-pine furniture. A small round table and two chairs stood by the window. And yet, though the square footage was probably the same as her own bedroom, this space felt small. Enclosed.

She stared at the corner where the ceiling met the wall. The three sharp right angles seemed to tighten and compress, closing in on her. Like a prison cell. Never before had Cara been claustrophobic. What was going on inside her mind? She shook her head. What was wrong with her?

The abduction had made her anxious and tense. No matter how much she denied her fears, they were there. Real. Unforgettable. Nightmare predators that could tear away her flesh and suck the marrow from her bones.

When a tap came on her bedroom door, she was glad for the interruption in her decidedly morbid thoughts. She sat on the edge of the bed. "Come in."

Dash entered with a tray in his hands. He kicked the door closed behind himself and carried the tray to the table. "You need to eat."

Her mood was dark, and she was still annoyed by the way he'd slipped out during her formal interview. "How do you know what I need?"

"Trust me." At the table, he unloaded two plates and two mugs. "The coffee is excellent."

She climbed off the bed and approached the table where Dash had set a plate of fresh green salad and lasagna, redolent with garlic and oregano.

"You're moving better," he said.

"My feet don't hurt as much."

"Tomorrow, you'll be seeing a doctor."

"No pills," she said quickly. "Once these hallucinogens work through my system, I'll be fine."

"Not that kind of doctor. A shrink."

"Why?" She whipped around to face him. "Do you think I'm crazy?"

"Not unless you try to pretend that nothing happened. You've been through one hell of a trauma, Cara. It's only natural that you'd be feeling anxiety."

"I can handle it." She didn't want to be traumatized, didn't want to let this experience tear her apart.

He glanced toward Yazzie, who hadn't moved from the bed. "I didn't forget you, cat." Dash placed a small dish on the floor. "Albacore tuna."

Instantly, Yazzie pounced. After one sniff, he started snarfing up his dinner.

Cara knew she should do likewise. Her body needed food, but she had little appetite. She sat at the table, picked up her fork, then set it down again. "Why didn't you do the interview with me?"

"Because I was a part of what happened. Flynn was able to approach you with a fresh perspective."

"I didn't do very well in answering his questions. Couldn't remember with any degree of certainty."

"It wasn't a test."

"That's good because I would have gotten a D-minus."

"Not an F?"

"I never give a failing grade to someone who's really trying. And I was. Really." She exhaled a sigh. "It's frustrating to not be able to remember."

"That doesn't often happen to you. You're high functioning. Probably an A student since kindergarten."

Automatically, she became defensive. Being one of the smart kids had never been easy. "Is my intelligence a problem for you?"

"Hell, no. I like smart women. And your IQ is in the genius range."

"How do you know that?"

"FBI."

"Oh, right. You know everything."

"I like to think so."

He smiled broadly, showing a perfect row of straight white teeth. She liked the way his deep-set blue eyes crinkled at the corners. A hint of stubble marked the line of his jaw, but he still looked well-groomed. Even on a day like this—a day that had started at dawn when he'd rescued her outside the burning house—Dash was unruffled. Cool. Calm. His white oxford-cloth shirt with the sleeves rolled to the elbow wasn't even wrinkled. She wondered what it would take for him to get messy. What would he do if she grabbed the front of his neat white shirt and tore it open, sending buttons spewing in all directions?

The inappropriateness of that idea startled her. He was a Fed. She was his witness. That was all they had in common. Even though she was aching to be held, she wouldn't make the mistake of falling for him. She needed to be careful. Or was she being too careful? Was that the reason she was living alone with Yazzie?

She glanced over at the cat who instead of eating kept darting glances around the room to make sure no one would dare touch his dish of tuna.

Then she looked back at Dash. Though he sat at the table, he wasn't eating, either. His gaze held steady, and she knew that bringing dinner wasn't the only reason he'd come to her room. "Why are you here?"

"I thought maybe you'd want to talk about it. Russell. The captivity. Your escape. The whole damn thing."

"I already did." Tension wrapped more tightly around her, squeezing the air from her lungs. "I told Flynn everything."

"Those were the facts. Not the emotions. You must have been scared. And angry."

"Confused." She pushed away from the table and stood. "My brain kept going off on tangents. And it's still happening. I don't know how I'm going to sleep tonight."

"Maybe if you tell me—"

"And fall apart right here and now? No, thanks." Her fingers wrapped around the back of the chair, and she hung on tightly, needing an anchor. "I'm fine."

"I read your narrative," he said. "Russell held the knife to your face. Near your eyes."

"Frightening. Of course, it was frightening." She fought the trembling in her voice.

"You need to let go."

He had it all wrong. She needed control— the most intense control she'd ever exerted in her life. Otherwise, she would say things that she'd regret. She'd feel too deeply. The pain would devour her. "Leave me alone, Dash."

"Russell told you that you were being judged. What would happen if you weren't worthy?"

"You know the answer to that question."

"Say it."

"He'd kill me." A sob wrenched from her throat. "I didn't want to die."

The predator demons she'd held at bay swarmed closer. She saw their fangs, dripping with blood. Heard their cries, rising louder and louder over a drumbeat.

She shrank back on the bed with her wrists held together as if she were still bound. Her hands covered her mouth, holding back a scream. "I don't want to die alone."

"You're not alone." Dash sat on the edge of the bed. His hand rested on her shoulder. "I'm here."

His touch released a torrent of words. "If I died, no one would miss me. Not my father who I haven't seen in years. I don't even know where he lives." Tears oozed from her eyes and drenched her cheeks. "And my mother." She gasped, unable to catch her breath. "If I died, my mother would be sad. So would my half sisters and my stepfather. Oh, sure they'd think of me. Once a year, they might put a rose on my grave. But their lives would go on. I don't have a family of my own."

He gathered her up in his arms, holding her gently against his chest while she cried. Whether from fear or anger or sadness, she didn't know. Being close to death had reminded her of all the things she'd been missing. All the dreams left unfulfilled.

"Is that what you want, Cara? A family?"

"More than anything."

She wanted the whole package—the perfect family. A house with a rec room, a TV, entertainment center, maybe a Ping-Pong table. She wanted to make dinner and afterward help the kids with their homework. She wanted a loving husband. Someone to share with. Someone who put her at the center of his world.

Somehow, she'd always thought that after her career was on track, she'd find that family. That one special man. "I want to belong with someone. Before death takes me."

"You're not gong to die," Dash said. "You're safe now."

"Am I? You said it yourself. Russell is obsessed. He won't stop until he finds me."

"No one can hurt you here," he said firmly. "There's electronic surveillance all around this house. Three armed federal agents. Four, including me."

She was safe in his arms. Gradually, her sobs lessened to small hiccups. She should have been embarrassed by her lack of self-control. Instead, she was tired. Everything she'd been holding inside had poured out.

She nuzzled against his damp white shirt, content to rest there until morning.

OVER BREAKFAST, DASH KEPT an eye on Cara. Last night, he'd stayed in her room until she'd fallen asleep. Even then, he hadn't left her. He'd pulled together a bunch of blankets, made himself a bed on the floor and spent the night listening to her breathing. Twice, she'd awakened. Each time he'd held her, chasing her nightmares away with his presence. It was the first time he'd spent the night in a woman's bedroom without making love.

But that wasn't what Cara needed.

His efforts had paid off. She was a different person this morning. Her appetite was back. She'd asked for seconds while chatting easily with the other agents and the other protected witnesses. She was charming. When she laughed, she was so damned beautiful that she made his heart ache. He was sorry for all she'd been through and glad that she was feeling better.

After the plates had been cleared, he took one last mug of coffee and escorted her into the den on the first floor where she'd done her interview with Flynn the previous night.

He closed the door. They were alone.

Cara wasted no time in coming to the point. "About last night," she said. "I don't usually—"

"You don't need to say anything."

"You were right, Dash. I needed to let go."

Being right wasn't the reason he'd gone to her bedroom. "The drugs should have worked through your system now. No more hallucinations."

She stepped toward him, fitting herself into his arms for a hug. Last night, he'd held her, but it wasn't like this. Her lithe body pressed against him, arousing thoughts he shouldn't be having about a witness.

Her head tilted back to look up at him. "Thank you."

"It's okay."

"Did you get any sleep at all?"

"Plenty. I'm used to keeping watch on stakeouts."

Her full lips parted. Her back arched, and she rose up on her toes, bringing her face closer to his. Her skin was smooth, unblemished. Her dusky complexion reminded him of a cool night. Only a few inches away from his mouth, her eyelids closed. Her black lashes formed delicate crescents above her high cheekbones.

He shouldn't kiss her. It wasn't professional. But Dash had never in his life wanted anything more.

His head dipped and his lips touched hers. Lightly. Cautiously.

A wave of sensation rocked through him. Her mouth pressed harder, and he responded. Dash was no longer an FBI agent comforting a witness. He was a man who wanted and needed contact with this incredible woman. Her body fit perfectly against him. Her mouth was warm, sensual and welcoming. And he felt something more. Something that stirred his blood. This kiss marked the beginning of the rest of his life.

He wanted to be with her forever, to be the man she belonged with. But that wasn't why he'd brought her to this room. He still had an investigation to pursue.

Reluctantly, he separated from her. "You look good this morning."

"Only good?"

"Damn good." His gaze slid up and down her body, taking in her azure blouse and silver jewelry. Earrings. And cuff bracelets. "But that's not what's on my mind right now."

She cocked her head, and her long black hair fell gracefully past her shoulders. "What's up?"

The FBI had been informed that Russell's father, William Graff, was in nearby Durango. By all accounts, he was a genuine pain in the butt—a wealthy man with a battalion of lawyers whose intention was to create barriers to the investigation of his son. He refused to help in the manhunt, refused to talk to law enforcement until he met with the woman who accused his son.

Flynn and Dash had discussed the possibility. William Graff might have information useful to their search. After he talked to Cara and saw that she was a reasonable person, he might open up. But Dash hated to put her in that position. She was at the safe house. In protective custody.

He didn't want to subject her to further trauma. And yet, she was key to finding Russell.

"Dash, what is it?"

"I had some questions about the people Russell was working with at that archaeological dig." He pointed her toward the sofa, where they sat side by side. The taste of her kiss still lingered, and he was having trouble being coherent.

"Have you spoken to anyone at the site?" she asked.

"On the phone."

He'd contacted the professor in charge, Dr. George Petty. Questions about Russell had resulted in very little useful information. The professor had described Russell Graff as a good kid, a diligent worker, very meticulous. "Another agent went to the site and did interviews. Supposedly, Russell has a girlfriend. Joanne Jones."

"I know her." Cara's voice was bright and confident. "I had her in class. A redhead. Kind of a marginal student. I was surprised when George selected her for the dig."

"Tell me about George. Is he the kind of guy who pals around with his students?"

"Not a bit. He's in his sixties and consumed by his work. Though romances tend to crop up at these sites, it's not a party atmosphere. No drinking. No smoking." She hesitated for a moment, thinking. "Dr. Alexander Sterling is at this dig. He's a forensic anthropologist. One of a handful in the country. Brilliant man."

Dash noticed that when she referred to Dr. Petty, she called him George. With Sterling, she'd used his title. A sign of respect. "Tell me about Sterling."

"As I said, brilliant. His comparative

analysis of skeletal remains on North American natives has led to a new hypothesis on…"

Blah, blah, blah. Dash couldn't care less about archaeological data. But obviously, Cara did. As he watched her rattle on about occipital bones and cranial capacity, her expression brightened. Her cloudy gray eyes shimmered with an enticing glow.

She gestured enthusiastically, pointing to her forehead and measuring her chin using her fingers as calipers. His gaze lingered on her mouth. For a moment, he wanted to yank her into his arms and silence her lecture with another kiss.

"…I'm surprised you haven't heard of Dr. Sterling," she said. "I believe he's been involved in some FBI matters."

Ironically, Dr. Alexander Sterling had been called in to offer an opinion on the Judge serial murders in San Francisco. "I'm aware of his reputation. I want your opinion of him as a man, someone who associated with Russell and might be able to tell us something about him."

"Dr. Sterling might be helpful in explaining the ritual aspects of Russell's behavior." She frowned, and her excitement disappeared behind a cloud. "When he held me captive, there was some sort of ritual. If I could remember the details, I could tell you more."

"That brings me around to something else we need to talk about. Dr. Jonas Treadwell is a psychiatrist who has had a lot of success in leading witnesses through reenactments of the crime. He doesn't use hypnosis, but he takes you through the details."

"Like what?" She seemed hesitant.

"Maybe you heard Russell mention a specific place. Or you saw a map or note he'd written. Clues that could help us find him. Are you willing to give this a try?"

"I'll try." The very last thing Cara wanted was to plunge back into the emotional content of her abduction. The pain. The fear. The humiliation. But she truly did want to help the investigation. "Will you stay with me?"

"I'll be in the room, but I won't interfere in the process."

"Let's do it. The sooner Russell is caught, the sooner I can get back to my regular life."

"He's with Flynn." Dash stood. "I'll tell them we're ready."

He left her sitting on the beige suede sofa in the den. Facing her were two matching chairs. At the far end of the room was a desk with a computer. Every wall was lined with bookcases. A long window overlooked the front porch. Like most of the other rooms in the house, the atmosphere was neat, comfortable and very masculine. There were no knickknacks, no plants or flower arrangements, nothing that would suggest a woman's touch. This was a houseful of men—FBI agents who weren't interested in making things pretty.

Dr. Jonas Treadwell fit that mold. Though probably in his fifties, his muscular shoulders suggested that he worked out on a regular basis. His hair was sun-bleached, his complexion tanned. When he shook her hand, his gaze confronted her directly.

"I'm pleased to meet you, Cara. May I ask if you've ever had therapy before?"

"While I was finishing my doctorate, I went to a psychiatrist twice a week." Telling herself that she had nothing to be ashamed of, she glanced toward Dash who had taken a seat in one of the chairs opposite the sofa. "We were dealing with stress. And with abandonment issues."

Treadwell gestured for her to sit on the sofa. "You felt abandoned by your father."

"That was a fact. Not a feeling. He left when I was four, and I never saw him again."

"Did you stay in contact with anyone else in his family? I know you're involved in Navajo tribal politics."

"His parents—my grandparents—passed away before he married my mother. Actually, I started working with the tribal council at the suggestion of my psychiatrist. It helps me stay in touch with my heritage." She reached up and tucked a strand of hair behind her ear. "I've worked through most of my abandonment issues."

"Have you?"

Of course, there was that issue last night about her desperate need to find a good man and settle down. She hadn't really acknowledged those feelings until the words had spilled through her lips. "Mostly."

He went to the desk, picked up a large tablet and brought it to her. He placed a charcoal pencil in her hand. "While we're talking, I'd like for you to doodle."

"Doodling?" A strange request. She couldn't imagine what a bunch of scribbles were supposed to accomplish. "Okay, you're the expert."

He sat in the chair opposite her and turned

to Dash. "I have a job for you, too. I want you to read Cara's written account of what happened. Sentence by sentence. Start now."

The sound of Dash's baritone voice reading her written words disconcerted her. There wasn't the slightest hint of fear in his tone as he read about her coming home from work, opening her door and checking her e-mail.

Treadwell gestured for Dash to stop. To Cara, he said, "Draw me a picture of your house. Or of one object in the house."

She started with the dining-room table. A rectangular surface cluttered with books and papers. Before she was really aware of what she'd drawn, Cara had sketched an aloe vera plant in a brown-and-white pot. When she'd finished, the sheet of paper was almost full.

At the far left edge, she sketched in the hallway arch leading toward her bedroom. The place she'd seen Russell standing. But she didn't want to place him there. Instead, she scribbled over that space until it was solid black.

"Tell me about what you've drawn," Treadwell said.

She described the room, noticing details that she hadn't been aware of before. The shock of seeing Russell in her house came back to her full force.

The memory generated a searing heat deep within her. She began to sweat. Instinctively, she looked toward Dash. His steady strength reassured her. He would protect her. He wouldn't let anything bad happen to her.

When Treadwell nodded, Dash read again from her written account of when Russell had attacked her with the stun gun.

"How did he get into your house?" Treadwell asked.

"The window." She could hear Russell's voice. "He apologized for breaking my window. He was shy. Almost as scared as I was."

"Did you see the broken window?"

"No."

"What did you see? Draw it."

Step by step, Treadwell lead her through the abduction. She filled several pages with lines and scribbles that were becoming more and more abstract. She couldn't stop drawing. The edge of her hand was blackened by charcoal.

She remembered the small square room of her prison. The drugged water bottle.

"Spiders," she whispered. "I know they weren't real, but I saw hundreds of spiders."

On the table were ritual objects. With furious strokes, she drew them. An eagle feather. A bowl of corn maize. A ceremonial pipe. The knife. Sage branches.

She dropped the charcoal pencil as if it had suddenly become red-hot. "I know what he was doing."

Chapter Six

Dash watched as Cara rose from her chair and began to pace, so excited that she wasn't even limping on her injured feet. Maybe she'd come up with a clue, a glimmer of memory that would lead to Russell's hideout.

She faced him and Treadwell. Her gray eyes fringed by thick black lashes actually seemed to sparkle. When she gestured, her silver bracelets flashed.

In a clear voice, she said, "The eagle feathers are important. The Hopi myth of Man Eagle is the story of a serial killer."

What the hell was she talking about? Now wasn't the time for a lecture on Native American history.

But Treadwell, the supershrink, nodded encouragingly. "Tell us the myth."

"Man Eagle captured many women from the tribe and killed them. Any person who entered his lair and attempted to save them was never heard from again, until he kidnapped the young wife of Son of Light who was clever enough to enlist the aid of magical beings like Spider Woman and Mole."

Though watching Cara was a treat, Dash didn't give a damn about Spider Woman and her mythical friends. Not when he had a *real* killer to catch.

She continued. "When Son of Light faced off with Man Eagle, there were several tests to determine who was superior. The winner got the girl. One test involved seeing who could eat the most."

"Hence the corn maize," Treadwell said.

"Others were feats of strength, tearing trees from the earth and breaking tree limbs. Which might be represented by the sage branches."

"Go on," Treadwell encouraged.

"The final competition," she said, "between Man Eagle and Son of Light was a trial by fire. Man Eagle had a magic shirt made of arrowheads that would protect him from heat. But Son of Light switched shirts with him. When Man Eagle stepped into the blaze, he was burned."

Treadwell seemed fascinated. "The way the Judge has burned all his victims."

"Russell must have been acting out his own version of this story. He spoke of tests, of how I could prove myself worthy."

"Wait a minute," Dash said. "The woman wasn't being tested. According to your story, the trials were between this other guy—Son of Whatever—and Man Eagle."

"It's a myth. Open to many interpretations." She met his gaze. "Maybe Russell is sending a message to you. Not you, personally. But to law enforcement. Challenging someone to step forward and face him."

"That fits the Judge's profile." Now Dash was interested. He remembered Flynn's comment about how the Judge had taunted him and enjoyed matching wits. "Some of his thrill comes from outsmarting law enforcement. What's the moral to this story?"

"Man Eagle was a monster," Cara said. "But he was also invincible. He could take any woman he wanted. No one could stop him until he faced the Son of Light."

"And was killed."

"In the end, Man Eagle was redeemed," she said. "After he had been burned to ashes, he was brought back to life as a good man."

Dash was interested in the story, but he had hoped that her memories might provide more tangible clues. License-plate numbers. A matchbook with a logo. A business card.

Treadwell didn't share his disappointment. The shrink was nodding like a bobble-head. "Russell sees himself as a monster. He asserts his power by kidnapping women and putting them through a ritual death that feeds his ego and, at the same time, promises ultimate redemption for him. I suspect that he endured an abusive childhood."

Dash scoffed. "I've heard plenty of versions of this story. Pity the poor monster—he can't help what he does."

"That's not what I'm saying." Treadwell shot him a vaguely hostile gaze. "Childhood abuse and trauma doesn't always result in criminal behavior. Nor does it excuse serial killing. There's always a choice."

"Why a Hopi myth?" Dash asked.

"The Native American myth is specific to archaeology—Russell's field of knowledge."

Which didn't provide any new clues or information. Russell was still invisible in spite of the manhunt that was underway right now in the Santa Fe area. "What do you think, Dr. Treadwell? Will he take another victim?"

The psychologist ran his hand through his sun-bleached hair that was beginning to thin in the back like a monk's tonsure. His gesture was nervous but his manner was smug. Like so many experts, he thought he had all the answers.

"I'm not sure. He hasn't yet finished with Cara."

"What do you mean?"

"None of the Judge's other victims have escaped. My assumption is that Russell will come after Cara again. She's a threat to his omnipotence."

Cara returned to the sofa. Her lips pressed tightly together. Clearly, this wasn't what she wanted to hear.

Nor did Dash. "What else can you tell us about Russell?"

"As I mentioned before, there was probably childhood trauma. We know Russell was adopted at age five, and his early days may have affected his behavior. It would be useful if you could speak with his adoptive parents."

Finally, Dash had a course of action. Russell's father was in Durango, only thirty miles from here. And he had demanded to meet with Cara. Not that William Graff had the right to make demands, but suddenly it became a useful excuse.

Dash would exhaust all other possibilities before asking this of Cara. Involving her in the active investigation went against all the rules. But it might be the only way.

AFTER LUNCH ON THE FOLLOWING day, Cara stepped into the sunlight of a brilliant spring day. She turned back toward the safe house and blew a farewell kiss to Yazzie who had taken up permanent residence on the windowsill of her second-floor bedroom, then she climbed into the cab of a truck. Though leaving the safe house, she felt very well-protected, sandwiched between two federal agents. Flynn was behind the wheel. Dash sat to her right. Both men were armed and potentially dangerous to wrongdoers.

There was nothing to be afraid of. Last night, she'd slept well. Her wounds were healing; it was no longer painful to walk in shoes. With every hour that passed, she felt more like herself. In control. Steady. Stable.

Cara was under no obligation to help with the investigation. Both Dash and Flynn had made it crystal clear that she didn't need to come along on this visit to Russell Graff's father, even though the elder Graff had said that he wanted to talk with her, and her presence might encourage him to open up.

How could she refuse? She wanted Russell caught. If there was any way to help, she wouldn't say no.

Dash reached toward the knob on the radio that was playing country-western music. "Mind if I change the station?"

"Yes, I mind," Flynn said. "I like this music."

"You've really gone cowboy. The Stetson. The boots. The whole damn thing." Through his FBI-issue dark glasses, Dash glanced toward Cara. "Would you believe this guy grew up in west Los Angeles?"

Flynn looked like the archetypal cowboy. He even had the squint of someone accustomed to staring at the distant horizon. She said, "People have the right to change."

"That's called personal growth," Flynn said. "Something Dash knows nothing about."

Dash slid his thumbs down the lapels of the navy-blue sports coat he wore over a white shirt and Levi's. "Are you giving me a hard time because I'm dressed like a grown-up?"

"An adult?" Flynn scoffed. "You still look

like a spoiled little rich kid who graduated cum laude from Harvard Law School."

Cara was surprised. "You went to Harvard?"

"It was a long time ago."

A lot of men would have worked that prestigious bit of information into the conversation right after hello, but Dash had neglected to mention his education. He didn't like to talk about himself. So she turned to Flynn. "What do you mean when you say he's a rich kid?"

"Adams is a common name," Flynn said. "But Dash can trace his roots back to a couple of presidents of the United States. In fact, I think his middle name is Quincy. Dashiell Quincy Adams. His family had deck chairs on the *Mayflower*."

"No big deal," Dash muttered. "That and four bucks will get me a latte at Starbucks."

"The difference is," Flynn said, "you could buy your own Starbucks. His family is a bunch of rich lawyers. Dash was prep school and polo games all the way."

Dash shifted uncomfortably beside her, and his thigh rubbed against hers, reminding her of their more intimate physical contact. She'd never kissed a rich man before, and she had to wonder if it would ever happen again. He'd barely spoken to her since yesterday. "Did you wear one of those little jackets with a crest over the pocket?"

"Enough about me," he said. "We should discuss what we're going to say to Russell's father."

"He's rich, too." Flynn grinned. "You should do the talking, Dash. You can relate to the upper crust."

"His family wasn't wealthy," Dash said. "William Graff has a successful import/export company based in San Francisco, but the business was mostly financed by money from his wife's family."

"Old money?" Flynn asked.

"Nob Hill," Dash confirmed. "She's active in charities. Helping the homeless. They adopted two disadvantaged kids. Russell when he was five. Another boy from infancy."

"Sounds like an admirable thing to do," she said.

"Don't get your hopes up," Dash warned. "Good intentions don't always lead to good results."

"Why is Mr. Graff in Durango?"

"He has connections there, and he wants to be in this area because he doesn't believe that his son—who's had every advantage money can buy—would turn out to be a serial killer."

That had to be a parent's worst nightmare. She almost felt sorry for William Graff. "Do you have any idea why he wants to talk to me?"

"Intimidation," Dash said. "Though I'd like to think William Graff was looking for the truth about his son, I suspect he'll try to browbeat you."

Cara straightened her shoulders. Nobody browbeat *her.* "And what do we hope to gain from this meeting?"

"Two things," Dash said. "First, we want info on Russell. Second, we want his father to understand that if Russell contacts him, he's required to turn over any leads to the FBI."

Dash's purpose seemed to be much the same as that of William Graff. Intimidation.

Not her favorite thing. She leaned back against the seat and watched the scenery go by. This part of southern Colorado wasn't all that different from the land surrounding Santa Fe. Mountains and mesas and hardy vegetation that could thrive in the arid climate.

Her gaze took a detour and came to rest on

Dash's profile. A Harvard man. A preppy. She wondered which of his illustrious forefathers was responsible for those incredible blue eyes.

When he noticed her watching and turned toward her, she averted her gaze. There was something growing between them, but she wasn't sure if she could call it a relationship.

AT AN ATTRACTIVE LODGE on the outskirts of Durango, the three of them were ushered into a sitting room where William Graff was waiting. Though Russell was adopted, Cara saw a resemblance to the gray-haired man who glared as she entered the room flanked by Dash and Flynn. Like Russell, he was tall and thin. William Graff's mouth pulled into a severe grimace, and she realized that she'd seen that same expression on Russell's less mature face.

Dash stepped forward and exchanged handshakes with the senior Graff.

"I appreciate your willingness to meet with us," Dash said. "The sooner that we find your son, the better for everyone."

"Agreed," Graff snapped. "My son would never do these things you've accused him of.

The FBI is dead wrong, and I want this crap over with as soon as possible."

When Graff tried to approach her, Dash cut him off. "Please take a seat, sir."

He did as ordered, and Cara was glad not to be forced to shake his hand. There was something cold and forbidding about William Graff. When he looked at her, she could feel his disapproval. She and Flynn remained standing while Dash sat in an armchair beside Graff and leaned forward attentively.

Dash got down to business. "When was your last contact with Russell?"

"He called home a week ago. Seemed to be enjoying his time at the dig site. Why he chose something as useless as archaeology for a major, I'll never know." He shot a glare at Cara. "You gave him an A in the class you taught."

She nodded. "Russell was a good student."

"You liked him," Graff said.

Before she could respond, Dash said, "Sir, can you tell me what you and Russell talked about when he called?"

"Nothing important," he growled. "The weather."

"Where was he when he called?"

"Hell if I know. He was on his cell phone."

"Can you tell me what kind of vehicle he drives?"

"He has a Ford Explorer. Dark green. I gave it to him on his twenty-first birthday. He needed a vehicle capable of going off-road since he's determined to pursue a career that takes him to godforsaken locations."

"Russell went to high school in San Francisco," Dash said.

"That's right. Private school."

"Did he participate in after-school activities?"

"He's not antisocial. If that's what you're getting at. Russell is a marathon runner. Like me." Again, he looked past Dash toward her. "He got decent grades. Not good enough for an Ivy League school. But decent."

"Did he—"

William Graff interrupted, "Once he had a crush on a teacher. She looked a little bit like you, Cara."

Did he kidnap her, too? She swallowed to keep from blurting out a statement she might regret.

Dash spoke for her. "Did he tell you about this crush?"

"He mentioned it. Said his teacher was

more interesting than the girls his own age. She was worthy of his attention."

Again, Cara stifled her response. Russell had said the same thing to her. She had to prove herself worthy.

"And what happened?" Dash asked. "Was he ever actually involved with this teacher?"

"The boy was only fifteen, and I wasn't about to let him have an inappropriate affair." Graff's scowl deepened. "I had the bitch fired."

"I see," Dash said tersely. "Were there other women?"

William Graff stood and pointed at Cara. "That's what I should have done with you. I should have had you fired for seducing my son."

She couldn't stay silent. "My relationship with your son was professor to student. Nothing more."

"I don't believe you, Cara."

"Dr. Messinger," she corrected him coldly. "Call me Dr. Messinger."

"You got my boy into trouble, didn't you?"

She knew he was baiting her. His allegations were baseless and absurd, but she couldn't hold back. "Your boy—as you keep calling him—broke into my house."

"You're lying."

"You're blind," she fired back. "You couldn't see how troubled Russell was."

"Don't blame this on me. I raised him the right way. Adopted him, gave him everything." He took another step toward her. "You're the problem. You dragged him off for a little rendezvous, didn't you?"

"I most certainly did not ask for—"

"That's what this is all about." He took another step toward her, raised his arm and pointed an accusing finger. "You had an affair with a student and now you're trying to cover it up. Your word against his."

Dash grabbed his wrist, spun Graff around and twisted his arm behind his back.

Graff yelped. "Take your hands off me."

"I suggest you settle down, Mr. Graff."

"Who the hell do you think you are?"

"FBI. Don't threaten me or my witness."

"Or else what?"

"Federal prison," Dash said as he released his hold.

Graff stumbled away from him. His face contorted with rage. "You have nothing to connect Russell to these other murders. Nothing but the word of this…woman."

When Dash reached into his inner coat

pocket, Cara thought for a moment that he was going for the gun in his shoulder holster. Instead, he pulled out a rectangular silver case filled with business cards.

"Your son," Dash said, "is a fugitive. If you or your wife have any contact with him, you will contact me."

"And if I don't?"

"I'll take great pleasure in arresting you or Mrs. Graff for aiding and abetting. And obstruction of justice." He flipped the card toward Graff's chest and turned on his heel. "Good day, sir."

With Flynn, they walked from the room and down the hallway. Cara's pulse raced, pumping adrenaline through her veins and heightening her senses. She wasn't accustomed to the FBI methods of conversation but appreciated the way Dash came to her defense. It might be useful to learn how to do that arm-twisting thing.

"Nice job," Flynn drawled. "Real subtle."

"I perceived a threat," Dash muttered. "He's lucky I didn't break his arm."

In the paneled front lobby opposite the reservation desk, Cara saw something that caused her to halt. On a side table beside a flowering cactus was a ceramic bowl. The

black-and-white pattern of interlocking rec-
tangles resonated in her memory.

"What's wrong?" Dash asked.

She pointed. "That bowl looks exactly like
the one that was in the room where Russell
held me captive. It was filled with maize."

"Are you sure?"

She couldn't be positive. The pattern was
similar to many others from the southwest-
ern tribes, especially the Ute. "It looks like
the same one."

"Okay," Flynn said as he turned toward
the reservation desk. "We can take this bowl
as evidence. There might be fingerprints."

Outside, she inhaled a breath of fresh
mountain air, hoping to clear her mind and
rid herself of the ugliness she'd felt when
confronted by William Graff. She wanted to
get away from here and quickly followed
Dash into the parking lot.

"I owe you an apology," he said. "I
shouldn't have subjected you to this."

"I'm glad you did." She walked faster to
keep up with him. "Now I have an idea of
what to expect. Is what William Graff said
true?"

"About what?"

"Evidence," she said. "Is my testimony

the only thing connecting Russell to these other crimes?"

"If Russell actually is the Judge, you're the only link. The other victims are dead, their bodies incinerated. We've never found DNA or fingerprints."

"So Russell might *not* be the serial killer."

At the truck, Dash opened the door for her. "Proving the case isn't something you need to worry about. What Russell did to you is enough to have him locked up."

But it was only her word against Russell's. Though she'd never done anything to lead him on, the implication was there. Like William Graff, people might think she'd encouraged Russell, that she wanted his sick attentions. "I hope this never comes to trial."

"Why not?"

"You heard what he said. That I'm some kind of tease." If William Graff hired a dream team of high-priced lawyers, she'd be dragged through the muck. Every facet of her sex life—as boring as it was—would be put on display. "This is so wrong."

"If it goes to trial, I'll defend you," Dash said. "And I'm Harvard. Cum laude."

"That and four bucks," she said.

Flynn ran toward them. In one hand, he

held the ceramic bowl wrapped in a plastic bag. In the other was his cell phone. "Let's go. We've got to move."

"What is it?" Dash asked.

"They found another body. About forty miles west of here."

Chapter Seven

Dash hated riding shotgun, but he had to admit that Flynn was making good time. They'd left the highway and were following side roads through a land of mesa and canyon. In Dash's opinion, it was too damned much scenery—too much open space for a killer to hide.

Russell could be anywhere. If he knew his father was in town, he could be following them, coming after Cara. It was unfortunate that they didn't have time to take her back to the safe house, but that trip would have added more than an hour. He and Flynn needed to be at the crime scene as quickly as possible. Though Dash had nothing against local law enforcement, the FBI had the best lab in the country for handling forensic details, and they needed evidence.

William Graff had been correct when he'd said they didn't have tangible proof that Russell was the Judge. Though he signed his e-mails as the Judge and left fingerprints in Cara's house, there was no incontrovertible link with the prior murders. Their case against Russell boiled down to similarities, and Cara's testimony. Her word against his.

Dash glanced down at her. It was his job to keep her safe. Instead, he'd dragged her into a confrontation with William Graff, that abusive bastard. Living with him would be constant trauma. Dash was damn certain that Dr. Treadwell would say the elder Graff contributed to his son's psychotic behavior.

Cara looked up at him through her thick lashes. "Dash, are you all right?"

"I'm supposed to be asking you that question."

"You look worried," she said. "Are you thinking about the maize bowl?"

"Maybe." If Russell had left that bowl, his reason might be connected to his father. A greeting. Or a way of saying goodbye. A threat?

Dash was also bothered by the fact that this killing had taken place in Colorado instead of New Mexico. Though they were over forty miles away from the safe house, Russell was too close.

Flynn parked the truck on the shoulder of a two-lane road. Half a dozen other vehicles, including those of local police and park rangers were pulled off to the side. Flynn was quick to get out of the truck.

Dash stayed behind with Cara. "Don't leave the truck. Keep the windows up. Doors locked."

She tucked a strand of shining black hair behind her ear. "I want to come with you."

"Not a chance."

"Don't worry. I'll be safe."

Her gaze was steady, almost too calm. "Why are you so sure?"

"Because of where we are."

She pointed, and he turned to look. The afternoon sunlight outlined the shape of ancient cliff dwellings. The view was remarkable: a two-story stone house among several smaller structures tucked under the overhanging lip of a mesa. This village was perched on a ledge high above the ground. "How did they get up there?"

"You've never been to Mesa Verde before?"

"No."

"This is called the Balcony House." Her

voice slipped into professor mode. "An excellent example of stone-and-mortar construction. The only way to reach it is to climb a thirty-foot ladder and crawl through a tunnel."

"When was it built?"

"Around 1100 or 1200 AD," she said.

"The Middle Ages," he said. "Same time as the Notre Dame Cathedral was being built in Paris."

"I suppose so." She eyed him curiously. "Are you interested in European history?"

"Not really. Some things just stick in my head. I'm good with dates."

"Me, too." She flashed a conspiratorial grin. "You might be as big a nerd as I am."

"God, I hope not."

She laughed. "It might sound superstitious, but I always feel calm here. And safe."

"A spiritual thing."

"Not really," she said. "I'm Navajo and the cliff dwellings were built by the Pueblo or Anasazi. Although I guess I could call them ancestors. We're all *dineh,* the people."

Through the windshield, he saw a number of men in uniforms. Yellow crime-scene tape fluttered from tree branches. He was itching to join them, but he also wanted to stay here with Cara, listening to her lecture about the ancients.

He had never known anyone like her before. Obviously intelligent and ambitious enough to become a full professor in her twenties. Those were characteristics he could relate to. But she also had an otherworldly quality—a well-guarded, secretive inner life that made him want to peel away her defenses and know her completely.

"I guess," she said, "I feel peaceful here because I'm an archaeologist. Drawn to the past. When I'm working a dig site, I forget to eat. I don't want to sleep. It's completely intriguing. The centuries of human existence make my own problems seem small and trivial."

"I understand," he said. "Being at a crime scene is like that for me."

"Then let's go."

"Not a good idea." Though he would have preferred dealing with a more cooperative individual, he had to admire her grit. "I don't want to go into details, but this is a murder scene. With a corpse."

"I'm an archaeologist. I've dealt with human remains before."

"It's not the same," he said. "This victim hasn't been dead for years, buried in a tomb."

"I want to see the remains."

Her voice was clear and confident. Unafraid. He could hardly believe this was the same woman who had wept in his arms. "What about the nightmares?"

"Hallucinations. They came from my imagination. I need facts. I can't bury my head in the sand and pretend this isn't happening. I can't hide from what Russell is doing."

Though her request went against procedure, he understood her need. Cara had a right to know about the man who was after her. "You can come with me. But this is a crime scene, so don't touch anything."

He cracked open the door to the truck and escorted her down the slight incline to an open area in the midst of fir trees and juniper. He and Cara joined Flynn, who was talking to a uniformed officer.

Flynn squinted in her direction. "Are you sure you want to be here?"

"Yes."

"Okay." He turned to Dash. "This murder doesn't fit the pattern. The Judge holds his captives four days, and it's only been two since Cara escaped."

Dash was growing impatient with Flynn's insistence that Russell wasn't the Judge. "He's stepping up his timetable."

"It doesn't work that way," Flynn said. "There's a ritual involved with these murders."

"He never had a victim escape before," Dash pointed out. "Cara interrupted his regular procedure. He's making changes to adapt, set things right again."

"Maybe," Flynn said grudgingly.

Dash turned to the officer and asked, "Who found the body?"

"Park rangers. They spotted a fire, and this isn't a sanctioned camping area."

"Why here?" Flynn questioned. "Why in Mesa Verde?"

Though Dash had scoffed at Cara's story of Man Eagle, it made a certain amount of sense in this context. "There's a Hopi legend about a serial killer. Russell might be acting out that story, leaving his victim in the shadow of the cliff dwellings."

"As a challenge," Cara added. "He knew the body would be found when the rangers saw the fire."

"What kind of challenge?" Flynn asked.

"Between us and him," Dash said. "According to the legend, there was a series of contests."

Russell was playing a game where he was the only one who knew the rules. Dash turned to the officer. "Mesa Verde is a national park. Is there any check-in process?"

"This area includes over fifty thousand acres and a limited staff of park rangers. No cameras. No surveillance."

"Let's see the body."

At this point, he expected Cara to show some reaction. Instead, she remained stoic. Her delicate features betrayed nothing of what was going on inside her head.

Inside the yellow tape was a neat fire circle of rocks and a charred corpse. Like the other victims of the Judge, she was curled in a fetal position with wrists crossed below her chin and her knees pulled up. The earth beneath her wasn't burned, leading to the conclusion that she was already dead before he'd brought her here.

"We tried not to disturb anything," the officer said. "But you won't find much in way of footprints. The ground is too rocky and dry."

From four feet away, Dash studied the remains. The flesh had been burned away, leaving charred bones—an end result that was both macabre and strangely compelling.

"Fascinating," Cara said as she crouched down to get a better look. "Intense heat is required to incinerate human flesh. Yet he's taken care to maintain the integrity of the skeleton. He must have burned the body for hours in a fire pit or used a blowtorch to sear away the skin, muscle and organs."

He recognized the professorial tone in her voice. "What else do you see?"

"There's a ritual aspect in the posing of the body."

Cara wished she could move closer. She studied the remains as if they had come from an ancient grave site. Every culture since the beginning of time had rituals surrounding death. What would this dead woman tell her about Russell?

"The remains are female," she said.

"How do you know?"

"For one thing, the size." She noted the length of the shin bone. "She was probably about five-one or five-two."

She stood and faced Dash. "May I move closer?"

"Just don't touch anything."

Close to the bones, she squatted down. "The pelvic structure is female. I doubt she ever had children."

Cara studied the crossed wrists below the

jaw. The fingers curled into fists. Some of the smaller bones were missing.

"An adult," she said. "The cranium is fully formed. The occipital ridge is characteristic of a female."

The skeletal face stared back at her, and Cara felt her academic detachment crumble. Yesterday, this had been a living, breathing being. A woman with dreams and hopes. A woman like Cara herself.

Her heart ached when she thought of a young, vibrant woman who deserved a chance at life. This unnatural death had come too soon.

As she stared at the skeletal remains, the voices of the other people—the park rangers and officers, Flynn and Dash—became distant echoes. The wind stilled, and the afternoon sunlight took on a darker hue. Rather than deny it, she accepted the sensation. Her breathing became shallow. Her pulse slowed. She seemed to be alone with this woman on a different plane of existence.

Their fates ran parallel. Yet, Cara had escaped. This victim had died.

She wished for a way to mourn. Though she hadn't been raised on the reservation, the Navajo had many ways of sending the dead on their way. Chants and rituals. Burial mounds. Lodge burials. Silently, Cara offered a blessing of her own. *May you find peace.*

That wasn't enough. This woman had been murdered. *May you find justice.*

"Cara." Dash's voice called her back to this arid land within sight of the cliff dwellings. A special, mysterious place. She caught a gasp of air. Her lungs expanded within her rib cage. When she returned to her conscious body, she felt energized.

Rising, she faced him. "You were right. This is different than uncovering an archaeological site. More empathic."

"More real."

This was Dash's world. A place where violence was commonplace. She couldn't imagine how he could face these terrible things, day after day.

From outside the crime-scene circle, Flynn gave a shout. "There's something over here."

She and Dash joined him beside a flat rock. Protruding from underneath were two eagle feathers.

"Man Eagle," she said. "He left them as a signature."

"And this." Flynn pointed. "I don't want to

move it until the forensic people get here and take photos. Maybe you can identify it, Cara."

Beside the rock was a clay pipe with black and brown designs. "A ceremonial pipe. It looks like the one that was in the room where I was held."

"Evidence." She heard satisfaction in Dash's tone. "Even if there aren't fingerprints, the pipe could tie him to this murder."

Cara took a step back and waited while Dash and Flynn conferred. Turning her head, she looked toward the Balcony House, an ancient fortress where the *dineh* sought protection from their enemies. Inside those stone walls, no one could reach them.

She stood on her own battlefield, threatened by one man. But she wasn't alone. All these officers were here to protect her. And Dash.

His job was to keep her safe, and she trusted him. He'd spent a whole night comforting her. When nightmares threatened, he chased them away.

He rejoined her. "We'll leave Flynn here to supervise the forensics. I want to get you back to the safe house."

She offered no objection. "I've seen enough."

As they hiked up the hill toward the truck, she asked, "Why did you become a hunter?"

"A hunter? I don't think of myself that way."

Maybe not, but that was his identity within the tribe. He hunted the enemy and protected others. A hunter. A warrior. "A Fed, then. Why?"

"It's complicated."

She wasn't about to be put off with a quick disclaimer. She planted herself at the door to the truck and looked up at him. "From what Flynn said, you had a comfortable childhood. Then Harvard. Then what?"

His gaze darted. Clearly, he was uncomfortable talking about himself. "Why do you need to know?"

"I've placed my life in your hands. At the very least, I deserve a brief biography."

He exhaled a slow breath. "After Harvard, I did what my family wanted. Joined the family law firm. Got married."

"Married?"

"She was a beautiful woman. Great social skills. She would have made a better attorney than I ever was. After I quit the firm and joined the FBI, we grew apart. Divorced. No kids. And that's my brief biography." He pulled open the door to the truck. "Let's go."

"Not yet." She slammed the door shut. "I still want to know why you joined the FBI."

"For one thing, I'm not real good at riding a desk. I like a more hands-on approach."

Like the way he'd questioned William Graff. An attorney wouldn't have yanked the man's arm behind his back and threatened prison. "What's the other thing?"

"Murders like this one." A muscle in his jaw clenched. "No one can ever make something like this right. I can't give this woman her life back. But I can give her justice by finding her killer."

A worthy goal, and she wholeheartedly agreed. "I want to help."

He eyed her curiously. "I thought you were anxious to get back to your normal life and put this behind you."

"That was before I saw the victim." She would never forget her visceral connection to the dead woman. "I want the same thing you do, Dash. Justice."

"Which is why you need to stay safe. Your testimony is our best evidence." He took her hands in his. "The most important thing is to protect you."

She looked down at his fingers, laced with hers. He offered comfort, safety and a warmth that had nothing to do with the investigation. She knew that he cared about her. Whether or not either of them admitted it, their connection was deeper than that of bodyguard and witness. "Do you think he'll come after me?"

"He's obsessed with you."

"Maybe we should let him find me. That's one way to draw him into the open."

"Not a chance."

"You've got to stop him, Dash. Before he kills again."

"I'll find a way."

"Promise me that he'll be stopped."

When she lifted her gaze, she saw her own intensity reflected in the determined set of his jaw, but she knew he couldn't guarantee that Russell would be caught before another woman died.

Chapter Eight

That evening after dinner, Cara lingered over coffee at the long dining-room table in the safe house. Her thoughts bounced back and forth like a Ping-Pong ball. When she'd been talking to Dash, she'd offered to use herself as bait to draw Russell into the open. It was a good plan, and not completely irrational.

On the drive back, Dash had argued against anything that would put her at risk. When they'd arrived, he'd disappeared into the office area in the bunkhouse, claiming that he had reports to file. But he hadn't come out for dinner, and she suspected he was avoiding her. The big, brave FBI agent was hiding from her questions.

With the two agents who lived at the safe house in the kitchen cleaning up the dishes,

Cara was left at the table with the two other protected witnesses who were currently housed at this facility. One was a sophisticated-looking woman with a long gray braid. Her name was Grace Lennox, and she was a judge. The other was a wiry man with a bald head and sharp features—Bud Rosetti.

Though they weren't supposed to talk about why they were here, Bud had a lot to say about everything else. Mostly complaints about the food.

"Meat loaf," he grumbled. "I haven't had meat loaf since I was a kid and my mom was pinching pennies to feed seven of us brats."

"Seven boys," Grace Lennox said with a nod to Cara. "Bud has told me all about his family, and I tend to think of them as the seven little dwarves. Bud must have been Grumpy."

He cracked a grin. "Was there a dwarf named Sexy? Because that suits me better."

"Apparently," Grace said with an arch of her eyebrow, "we're still talking about fairy tales."

Cara hid her grin behind her mug and took a sip of cappuccino. Delicious. Though she agreed about the bland meat loaf, the coffee was excellent.

Bud's beady little eyes narrowed as he

studied her. "So what's your story? Are you Indian?"

"Half-Navajo." She was accustomed to rude inquiries from children and people who didn't know any better. Tonight, she looked more Native American than usual with a patterned vest over her white shirt and her hair hanging loose past her shoulders. "But I grew up in a city. Like you."

"So you don't do the dances and feathers and stuff?"

"I've been to powwows and ceremonies." More as an observer than a participant. Wryly, she added, "And I have a lot of turquoise jewelry."

Grace chuckled, catching the sarcasm that flew right over Bud's bald little head. Undeterred, he said, "Tell me about the Indian casinos."

"I hate them."

"C'mon. Your people have got to be raking in the dough with those little gambling palaces."

"We'll see."

The first casino on the Navajo reservation had opened only recently, and she was concerned about the effect on the people who lived nearby. Gambling wasn't part of her tribe's culture; an ancient Navajo myth warned against the danger of losing everything to a clever gambler.

Like many others, she hoped the casino would provide much needed revenue, but she feared the worst. Increased crime rate. Gambling addiction. Alcoholism.

Discussion about the social problems brought by the casino was the first priority for the tribal council meeting on Thursday in Window Rock. Only two days away. She was determined to attend.

Bud bounced to his feet. "I'm gonna watch TV. Anybody else coming?"

"Perhaps later." Grace smiled at Cara. "I was hoping for a few moments of civilized conversation."

"Suit yourself, ladies." Bud stepped away from the table. "This means I get control of the remote."

"You *always* control the remote," Grace said.

"Hey, I watched that penguin movie with you. Two hours about birds that can't even fly." He sneered, revealing sharp little teeth. "If we gotta do the Nature Channel, it better be shark week."

He trotted down the hall, leaving the two

women alone in companionable quiet. Some women felt the need to fill the air with birdlike chatter. Not Grace. With her long gray braid, she reminded Cara of the archetypal Crone, or elderly wise woman.

Savoring her frothy cappuccino, Cara relaxed. The furnishings in the dining room—like the rest of the safe house—showed a masculine simplicity. Plain surfaces. Very few knickknacks. The only wall decoration was an antlered deer head that loomed above the sideboard, looking down on their conversation.

The two women talked about the loneliness of being in protective custody, sequestered from family and friends, and their work. Grace missed her courtroom, and Cara was reminded that she needed to grade final papers and access the information on her computer so she could file those grades.

Then Grace mentioned Dash. "Such a handsome young man. He's quite taken with you, Cara."

"He's only doing his job. Protecting me."

But the memory of their kiss contradicted her words. In that moment, that perfect moment, they had connected. She remembered the strength in his arms when he'd embraced her. His warmth. His scent.

Despite her words, when she heard the kitchen door slam shut and the low rumble of Dash's voice as he talked to the men in the other room, a buzz of anticipation spread through her.

"I believe his interest is far deeper." Grace tapped her neatly manicured fingernails on the tabletop. "Or perhaps, I've been watching too many soap operas with Bud."

"Bud watches the soaps?"

"When there isn't a sporting event."

Though Cara murmured a response about men and their games, her attention focused on the door leading through a pantry to the kitchen. Any moment, Dash would walk through. And what did she expect? Fireworks?

They'd spent most of the day together. There wasn't any logical reason for her to have missed him, but she was practically drooling with expectation.

Dash strode into the dining room with a mug in his fist. The sight of him did not disappoint. Even at the end of a long day with exhaustion pulling at the corners of his mouth, the man looked great. It was his eyes—his silvery-blue eyes, filled with the promise of strength, laughter and…sex. When he looked at her, she began to melt.

Then she saw Yazzie following close at Dash's heels. The big orange cat swaggered with his tail high in the air. The fur on his haunches was filthy. Cara glared at both of them. "What have you done to my cat?"

"I didn't mean for him to go outside." Dash took a seat at the table beside her. "He slipped through the door and followed me to the bunkhouse."

Yazzie sprawled at her feet. If he'd had any feline self-respect, he would have been cleaning himself. But no. With his pink tongue, he lazily licked his whiskers.

"What has he been eating?"

"Might have caught a chipmunk," Dash said. It wouldn't do any good to reprimand the beast. Yazzie loved to hunt. He was constantly bringing her all sorts of disgustingly bloody trophies.

Apparently, her cat had found a way to keep busy. Cara needed to do the same if she hoped to hang on to her sanity. "I wanted to ask you when I could get my computer back."

"No problem. I can set you up right now."

"You can?"

"All the information is saved. I can plug it into one of the computers in the office." Leaning back in the dining-room chair, his long legs stretched out in front of him. He lifted his mug to his lips, took a sip and exhaled a long, contented moan. "This is one hell of a good cup of coffee."

This was a man who adored his caffeine. His sensual groaning sent her thoughts spiraling again toward sex, but Cara managed to focus. "Can I use my e-mail?"

"No."

"Why not?"

He lapped up another taste of coffee. "You're in protective custody."

She looked toward Grace for a more cogent explanation. "Do you understand why we can't use e-mail?"

"I believe there's some possibility that the signal can be traced to an area," she said. "Or you might say something that would betray your location, perhaps an innocent comment about the weather."

"Well, that's ridiculous. I'd be careful."

"But the killer wouldn't know that. They might go looking for your e-mail contacts."

"And those people would be in danger." That much she could understand. "What if I just read the e-mail?"

"No," Dash said. "This whole thing started with e-mails. Remember?"

She wouldn't soon forget Russell's veiled threats that had turned real. Finishing the last dregs of her cappuccino, she stood. "I'd like to use the computer now."

He held up his coffee. "Give me a chance to appreciate this excellent brew. It's been a long day."

Though he looked exhausted, his sexiness was undiminished, innate, recumbent. She was drawn toward him. If she didn't pull away soon, she might do something she'd regret. "Just point me toward the computers."

"As if I'd trust you not to answer your e-mails?" He hauled himself to his feet. "Let's go."

Before leaving the dining room, she smiled at Grace. "I enjoyed our conversation."

"As did I." The older woman cast an appreciative glance toward Dash's retreating backside. "Just like the soaps."

In the kitchen, Cara turned and spoke to Yazzie, who had followed them. "You stay here, Yaz."

He planted his furry bulk in front of the door, making it impossible to open.

Dash smirked. "He's not listening to you."

Yazzie was an outdoor cat, utterly independent. Cara scooped him off the floor. Not an easy task. He was twenty-plus pounds of limp weight. She glanced toward the refrigerator. "He might be hungry."

"Right," Dash said. "The cat is obviously malnourished and wasting away."

Yazzie hissed at him.

Cara resettled Yazzie's weight in her arms. "I don't feel comfortable about having him running loose. There must be coyotes around here."

"And hawks and owls. And bears in the mountains."

"I'll carry him to the office."

Though it was dark outdoors, the yard was well lit. Only a few yards away was the entrance to the whitewashed bunkhouse, a long building with few windows. Beyond the three cottonwood trees, she saw the big red barn.

Yazzie wriggled in her arms. With a few twitches, he wrenched free and hit the ground running.

"Yazzie." She chased after him toward the barn.

The barn door was ajar, and she raced inside. The smell of hay and horses overwhelmed her and her nostrils twitched.

When she looked up, she found herself staring into the barrel of a handgun.

Wesley, the agent holding the gun, quickly lowered his weapon. "Sorry."

"No problem," said Dash, who had come up behind her. "It's good to know you're alert."

"Can't be too careful," Wesley said.

The atmosphere at the safe house was so calm and homey that she'd almost forgotten the potential for danger. "Is there any reason to believe that Russell knows I'm here?"

"None," Dash said firmly. "But you're not the only witness under our protection." He nodded to Wesley. "You made the right move."

"Thanks, sir. I appreciate that," Wesley drawled then grinned. Like Flynn and the other full-time agent living at the safe house, he was dressed like a cowboy from the boots to the Stetson. She wondered how long it would take for Dash to adopt western garb. He was already wearing jeans with his tweed sports jacket.

She looked back at Wesley. "Did you see my cat?"

"That big orange guy? He's probably hanging around with the other barn cats. There's a real pretty little calico girl."

Yazzie had not only found something to keep him occupied, but he also had a girlfriend. "I'm worried that he might get lost."

"I'll find him," Wesley promised. "And I'll put him back in your room."

Behind his shoulder, a horse nickered. A beautiful animal. Sleek, black and shining. Cara approached the stall. "Can I pet him?"

Wesley raised an eyebrow. "Been around horses much?"

"Not really." She'd been riding exactly twice, which was enough for her to know that she wasn't cut out to be a horsewoman. She noticed there were six stalls on this side of the barn and two on the other. "How many horses do you have here?"

"Five. Soon to be six. One of the mares is about to foal."

Tentatively, she stroked the bristly coat. The black eyes of the horse glanced down at her, then he snorted dismissively, as if to tell her that she didn't know what she was doing. Stepping away from the stall, she wiped her hand on her jeans.

"I'm surprised," Dash said, "that you're not into horses."

"Because I'm half-Navajo?" She was willing to put up with stereotyping from

Bud. But not Dash. "Because all Native Americans spend their spare time riding bareback across the plains?"

"Because you grew up in Denver," he said.

"Denver is a major metropolitan area," she informed him. "We have stoplights and everything."

Ignoring her sarcasm, he offered, "I could teach you how to ride while we're here."

"Maybe." At least she'd come away from this protective custody situation having learned a new skill.

As she watched Dash with the black stallion, she pictured him on horseback with the wind in his face. Though she knew from experience that most cowboys didn't make good boyfriends, she felt a primal attraction to that breed of loners. Manly men. Like Dash. "Where did you learn how to ride?"

"Polo."

So much for the cowboy image. He was preppy through and through. "I'd like to get started with my computer."

"It's kind of late to be working."

"I'm a night person."

After another assurance from Wesley that he'd find Yazzie, they left the barn. Crossing the yard, they entered the bunkhouse, which was divided into two sections. On one half of the long building was a potbelly stove and six single beds, arranged like an army barracks. Through a door was the safe house office area, filled with high-tech surveillance equipment, four different computers and other devices Cara couldn't identify. The air trembled with an electronic hum. "This room doesn't look like it belongs here."

"That's the general idea," Dash said. "This place is supposed to be a farmhouse."

"I didn't notice any crops."

"The horses," he said. "If anybody gets curious, we tell them that we raise horses."

He went to a desk with a computer, unlocked the top drawer and took out a plastic case with a memory chip, which he plugged into the computer. With a few strokes on the keyboard, her regular menu was displayed.

Seated at the desk, she adjusted her hands to the unfamiliar keyboard and opened her documents. All the files seemed to be intact. "This is a huge relief. I have some research on here that I'd hate to lose. Can I use the Web?"

He leaned over her shoulder. Though he'd finished his coffee, the scent lingered on his lips. He pointed to the screen. "What's that one? Casino."

"Some research I've put together for the tribal meeting at Window Rock. Remember? You promised I could go."

"How about this file? Wedding."

"My half sister is getting married next month." It occurred to her that all her private documents and information had been scrutinized by FBI agents. "There's nothing nefarious about my computer information."

"I didn't say there was."

"Is it okay if I open my e-mail file and see what's there? I promise not to answer."

When he reached around her to tap on the keyboard, his arm brushed hers. If she leaned back, her head would rest against his shoulder. A lovely thought.

Abruptly, he stood. "Here's your e-mail account. Put in your password."

She plugged in the code she used on everything: the Navajo word for *the people. Dineh.* Followed by *321.* Her birthday.

The screen lit up with forty-seven new messages, but she saw only one signature line. An e-mail from the Judge. The message line said: U-R-MINE.

She recoiled and yanked her hands away

from the keyboard as if it were red-hot. This was how it had all started. With stalker e-mails. Turning to Dash, she asked, "Did you know about this?"

"Our people have been monitoring your e-mails, but this is new."

She stared at the screen, willing the message to disappear, knowing that it wouldn't. "I can't ignore this."

"Open it."

With an ominous click on the keyboard, she revealed the message: You've been bad, Cara. Others will be punished in your place. One a day until I have you.

Her blood chilled in her veins. She couldn't let other women die in her place.

Chapter Nine

Dash stared at the threatening message on the computer screen. It hadn't been there earlier when he'd reviewed her documents. Russell must have logged on moments ago. If this e-mail could be traced, they would have his location.

Using the safe house walkie-talkie, Dash contacted Wesley in the barn. In addition to working with horses and making great coffee, the younger agent was their resident expert on computers and electronic communication.

There were other procedures to be followed, other experts Dash should call in. Negotiation with a psychotic subject benefited from the skills of a professional psychologist like Dr. Treadwell. But the shrink wasn't staying at the safe house, and Dash didn't want to wait and take a chance on losing this slender thread that might lead to Russell. "I'll respond to him."

Cara stood and faced him. Tension shuddered through her, but she didn't look scared. Sparks flared like lightning from her stormy gray eyes. "Let me do it."

Putting her in contact with Russell, even via e-mail, worried him. He'd already made a mistake by letting her in on the Mesa Verde crime scene where she'd mistakenly gotten the idea that she might become a part of this investigation.

At the same time, having her write the response made sense. Russell Graff was accustomed to her patterns of speaking and writing. He might be more susceptible to Cara's voice, even on e-mail. "Are you sure you can handle this?"

"I want to," she said. "He's threatening to punish one person a day until he has me. I can't let that happen."

"Take a breath, Cara. Calm down."

Her nostrils flared as she inhaled. He saw anger in the jut of her chin and the hard line of her mouth. Fired by rage, she was fierce. And stunning. He'd follow this Amazon into battle any day.

"Sit down at the computer," he said. "Use your own words. Encourage him to write to you again, to keep the contact going."

Her slender fingers poised over the keyboard for only a second before she began to type.

Dear Russell,
I'm terribly concerned about you. In my mind, I keep seeing the brilliant young student who took my classes. Please, please, please don't hurt anyone else. You must turn yourself in. It's the only way you can be helped.
Stay in touch,
Cara.

"Wait," he said. "Ask if there's someplace you could meet him."

She added one more line. "How's that?"

"Perfect." He never would have thought to add the three *pleases.* "Send it."

She did as he asked and rose from the chair. Energy crackled all around her. In the white sterile room, she was a mesmerizing burst of color. Her black silky hair. The pattern on her vest. Her cheeks flamed with color.

"The woman at Mesa Verde," she said. "Was she his first victim?"

Her question puzzled him. "Not the first. He's been killing for years."

"I meant the first on this sick vendetta to punish one person a day. Tomorrow, he'll look for another. Damn him. I'll do *anything* to stop him from killing again."

Wesley rushed into the office, and Dash briefed him. "I want you to monitor these e-mails. Let me know if he answers."

At the computer, Wesley tapped his way through several databases and worked the connections. The best possible thing that could happen would be for Russell to respond. If they got a dialogue going, they could track his signal.

"Still no response," Wesley said.

It was too much to hope that Russell had been sitting at his computer waiting for Cara to answer. "How long do we wait?"

"It depends on Russell's location and how he made the connection. Could be minutes." Wesley shrugged. "Or hours."

"Let me know as soon as you hear anything." Dash turned to Cara. "If you want, I can load that memory chip with your documents into a laptop, and you can use it like a word processor in your room."

"Not tonight." She shook her head. "I'm too angry to concentrate."

She looked as if she might explode if he didn't get her cooled down. "Let's get out of here."

Outside, a breeze rustled the leaves of the cottonwoods. Though cool, the air held little moisture. In San Francisco, the mist penetrated through clothing and skin. In this high desert, the wind was a dry slap in the face.

"Smell that," Cara said.

"Dust?"

"The scent of sage and pine."

"Sounds like a cleaning product."

"You don't appreciate this land." Instead of climbing the porch steps to the kitchen door, she walked beyond the lights into the surrounding shadows. "Come with me. I have something to show you."

Though he didn't want a lecture about the charms of the western states, he wasn't anxious to go inside. The contact with Russell had stirred his blood and awakened his instinct for the hunt. He wanted to take action.

Following Cara around the corner of the farmhouse, he knew she felt the same way. The need for speed. She moved with determination, and he admired the way her jeans outlined her long legs and cupped her butt. Her black hair shimmered in the moonlight.

She walked all the way to the split-rail fence at the front of the property. This wide-open valley was sheltered by mountains that rose in jagged tiers to high peaks. Apart from the safe house, they were alone. But the night was far from silent. There was wind, and the nocturnal rustling of predators.

When she turned and faced him, he was struck by her natural beauty. She didn't smile; her anger was still too strong. She spread her arm in a wide gesture, taking in the full scope of the landscape. "This is something you'll never see in San Francisco."

"Empty space? Total desolation?"

"Look up."

His gaze lifted above the mountains to the dark skies where countless galaxies spanned the heavens. One hell of a light show. More stars than he could count.

"No clouds to get in the way," she said. "No ambient light to hide the view."

The stars appeared close enough to touch. Clear, sparkling diamonds. "There's Orion's belt. And the Dipper. I wish I could remember the names of the constellations.

My grandfather used to point them out to us kids."

She rewarded him with a surprised grin. "That might be the first time you've shared something personal without me having to drag it out of you."

"I had a great childhood." It was only as an adult that he'd disappointed his family by leaving the law firm and joining the FBI. "Tell me more about the stars."

"Every ancient civilization has mythology about the night sky. From Stonehenge to the Mayans."

"And the Navajo?"

"One of the creation deities, the Black God, wears a black mask with the Pleiades above the brow. He's associated with fire, and he placed the stars in the sky. They were all neat and in order until Coyote, the trickster, messed them up. That's only one of the stories. There are dozens more."

No doubt, she could lecture him all night, and he wouldn't mind standing here and listening. When she was giving information, she seemed more comfortable and confident than at any other time. "I suppose I could stand to hear another."

"I particularly like the stories where the

spirits of dead brothers rise into the skies and become stars. A star can live for eternity."

"I like that idea."

Her gaze lowered until she was staring into the red dirt below her sneakers. "We can't let this happen, Dash. One victim a day."

"There's a manhunt underway. Federal agents, local sheriffs and state police from all four states are looking for him."

"I want to do something."

He moved closer and wrapped his arm around her shoulders. She leaned against his chest without embracing him. Her body hummed with tension. A wisp of her hair tickled his chin.

With his thumb, he tilted her head up so she was looking at him. In her eyes, he saw the reflected glory of the night sky. "There's nothing I'd like more than to go after Russell with both guns blazing, but there's nothing we can do. He's invisible. A shadow."

"But he has a weakness." Her lips curved in a smile. "Me. I'm his weakness. His obsession."

"We talked about this before. I can't use you as bait."

"And I can't sit around doing nothing while Russell kills other people in my name. Use me."

Dash was tempted. If he could arrange a situation where she'd be thoroughly protected and yet visible, Russell might show himself. The tribal council meeting at Window Rock was the day after tomorrow, and he'd already made arrangements to drive her there with an escort of other agents. She wouldn't be at risk. He'd have her completely secure.

Her arms slid inside his sports jacket. Her gaze encouraged him to kiss her. Once before, he'd succumbed. But not again. It went against all the FBI rules to fondle a protected witness. "Did you know that out here we're probably in sight of the surveillance cameras?"

"What do you mean?"

"I'm sure you noticed the bank of monitors in the office. There are several cameras watching the safe house. Some are infrared. They can see in the dark."

"Spy cameras?" Her spine stiffened.

"It's important to keep an eye on what's going on here. To watch for intruders."

She purposely stepped away from his embrace, leaving him with an armful of air. "Good night, Dash."

He watched as she strolled up the walk to the porch. The front door opened as she approached. Apparently, the other agent had been observing them from the front windows. Lack of privacy was part of the deal at a safe house, and he wished he could take her somewhere else. Maybe to a five-star hotel with Egyptian cotton sheets and champagne on ice. A resort with a hot tub where they could soak and relax and forget about serial killers.

Leaning against the split-rail fence, he gazed up into the millions of stars, looking for a way out. For himself. And for Cara.

THE NEXT DAY, CARA SPOTTED several of the hidden surveillance cameras that were tucked away in corners, invisible unless you took the time to notice. She hated the idea of being watched. Her mood was edgy, tense.

Russell hadn't responded to her e-mail. He'd tossed out his threat and vanished into cyberspace.

All day, she'd watched the clock. Would he take another captive? One a day. Dash had promised to tell her of any developments. Though she didn't want to hear of another death, she needed to know.

In her room, she sat at the pine table by the window and sorted through the final term papers that had been picked up by FBI agents from her office at the university.

First, she worked her way through upper-level papers. A gratifying exercise. The archaeology majors had already learned the basics and were writing about more interesting topics. But she also taught an intro course with over forty students. These papers were mercifully short and much less than scholarly. She read a title aloud: "Egyptology, Graphology and Archaeology: Handwriting Analysis of the Rosetta Stone."

Not much research here. "But he gets an A for creativity. Right, Yazzie?"

The cat lay sprawled in the center of her bed. He'd spent the morning strutting around in the barn, and she suspected he was happy for this chance to sleep. Acting the part of the stud took more energy than he was accustomed to.

Not so for Dash, who was effortlessly studly, even when he was doing nothing more interesting than drinking coffee. He'd surprised her last night by mentioning his grandfather and his happy childhood. Was he secretly a family man? The kind of guy who could settle down? Yeah, right. No way could she imagine Dash mowing the lawn and taking out the garbage.

She shuffled the papers again. It was important to get this work done today. Final exam week at the university was over and the grades for these students needed to be filed. Tomorrow was the tribal council meeting in Window Rock, and she hated to be dragging along a stack of term papers. *Get to work.*

But thoughts of Dash distracted her. It simply wasn't fair for him to be so amazingly sexy. Intriguing. And so unreachable.

Now that she was aware of safe-house surveillance cameras, she had to keep her distance. Possibly that unnatural separation was the reason she was dying to touch him, to glide her hands over his muscular chest, to kiss him until they were both gasping. A forbidden attraction was so much more enticing.

As she stared down at the paper, the neatly typed words swam in her vision. Maybe she should just give all these students As and move on. Some things were more important than academics.

No way. Her life had always been about learning and school. She loved her career. Being a professor was hugely important. Wasn't it?

Ever since that night when she'd fallen apart in Dash's arms, she'd been thinking about family. Finding that one special man. Her priorities had changed. Once, she would have been happy with papers to grade, future lesson plans to consider and a summer of research in the field. Now, she wanted more.

She startled at the knock on her door. "Come in."

One look at Dash's face told her that he had bad news.

Bracing her hands on the table, she forced herself to stand like a defendant facing the verdict.

"It was a deputy sheriff in Utah," he said. "A man. Russell ambushed him with the stun gun, then shot him."

"Is he dead?"

"In the hospital," Dash said. "He's expected to recover. He was shot in the leg. No bones broken."

Relief poured through her. This time, the punishment wasn't death.

"A man?" she questioned. This was such a radical change in his usual pattern. "Are you sure it was Russell?"

"He had a message for you," Dash said. "It

went like this—'Tell Cara that tomorrow is another day.'"

He wasn't through killing.

Chapter Ten

The next morning, after a breakfast of huevos rancheros, cantaloupe and fantastic coffee, Dash showed Cara the camper van they'd use to drive to the tribal council meeting.

From the outside, it didn't appear to be much larger than an SUV. But inside, the camper was fully furnished and surprisingly roomy. The two seats facing the windshield were captain's chairs that swiveled around to face a fold-down table. In the back was a tiny sink, stove and fridge. There was other seating against the wall of the van. And a narrow bed. It was a mini-home.

"Very nice," she said. "Where did you get it?"

"FBI."

His standard explanation for so many

things. His version of the FBI was part law enforcement, part snoopy aunt, and part Santa Claus. "Was this camper just laying around? Waiting until someone happened to need it?"

"Our people have access to a lot of equipment."

"Very cool. And does it come equipped with special FBI stuff? Like a machine-gun turret on the roof or bulletproof glass?"

"The doors lock, and it's enclosed. One hell of a lot safer than a pup tent in a campground."

The plan was to stay overnight. Window Rock was across two state borders in Arizona, about 125 miles away. A three-hour drive.

While he stowed her overnight bag and his own gear in the rear, Grace Lennox strolled up to the passenger-side window and gave Cara a sly smile. "This camper is so very cozy. I suppose you'll be spending the night with Dash."

"Not in the same bed," Cara whispered.

"That's what they always say in the soaps. And in the very next scene, the happy couple is bare-chested and kissing under rather artistic lighting."

"You and Bud need to find something else to watch on television."

She winked. "Don't do anything I wouldn't do."

Cara had no conscious intention of pouncing on Dash and forcing him into a lip-lock, but if things happened to heat up, she wouldn't be averse to another kiss. Maybe two.

He slid behind the wheel and slammed the door with enough force to knock all the romantic notions out of her head. Though he was wearing jeans and a sweater instead of his official FBI suit and tie, he couldn't have been more uptight if he'd been clad in armor.

"Something wrong?"

"Taking you to this meeting might be a big mistake. It's dangerous."

She'd heard this song before. "And you don't want to take a chance on losing me. Or my testimony." She fastened her seat belt. "Sometimes, I think that's all I am to you. A piece of evidence."

"Most evidence is more cooperative." He guided the camper to the end of the long driveway and turned south on a two-lane road. "Most evidence can be bagged, tagged and locked up until the trial."

She gave him a wide smile. "That other evidence isn't as interesting as I am."

"Granted." A grin tugged at the corner of his mouth. "You're a lot more fun than fingerprints and fibers."

"Not much of a compliment. Want to try again?"

He allowed his grin to blossom into a full smile. "You look very nice today."

She was dressed appropriately for a council meeting in a brown pantsuit with a coral shirt. Around her throat, she wore turquoise beads that matched the stone in her cuff bracelet and her dangling earrings.

"Much better," she said. "Thank you."

He nodded acknowledgment and turned to stare though the windshield. Though they could be driving straight into disaster, it felt good to leave the safe house. At least they were doing something. "What's our plan?"

"We drive south to Shiprock where we'll pick up another couple of agents in a second vehicle. They'll follow us to Window Rock."

"I hope you're not planning to come to the tribal council with me." The octagonal meeting room was huge, with plenty of room for eighty-eight delegates and spectators, but she really didn't want an FBI entourage. "You'll be bored silly."

"I'm not letting you out of my sight."

She tried a different tactic. "It's really not allowed for outsiders to—"

"I have permission. I've already explained the situation to the tribal cops, and they're willing to let me carry a handgun on the reservation."

She hadn't even considered the jurisdictional issue. Technically, the reservation was a sovereign nation that didn't fall under the purview of the FBI.

"A lot of precautions," she said. "Do you really think Russell will show up?"

"He might." Even behind his sunglasses, she could tell that Dash was scowling. "I'm not using you as bait, but it has occurred to me that Russell might know about your plan to attend this meeting. He might try something. If he does, I'm armed. And I have backup. No way will he get away from three federal agents."

"Can I have a gun?"

"Do you know how to shoot?"

"Not a bit."

"Then forget it," Dash said. "How are you coming with those papers you've been grading?"

It was an obvious change of subject, but she didn't mind. While they drove south into an arid landscape of mesa and canyon, she talked about the more interesting research subjects, including the site where Russell had been working. "An intricate cliff dwelling with signs of an irrigation system on the land below."

"Like Mesa Verde," he said.

"There are enough differences to make it unique, including communal burial mounds. That's a possible indication that several people died at the same time. Maybe in an epidemic. Maybe a famine."

She checked his expression for signs of apathy, not wanting to force him to listen to an archaeology lecture. But his interest seemed sincere. At least, he was asking all the right questions.

To their west was the Chuska mountain range, but this terrain was relatively flat. The road shot straight across the sparse landscape. In the distance, she spotted Shiprock—a jagged, natural monument of stone, rising fifteen hundred feet high. It looked like the prow of a ghostly ship sailing across the plains, hence the name.

Dash saw it, too. "How the hell did that get there?"

"This is a volcanic field. Shiprock is the neck of a volcano." She knew the geology but preferred a more poetic explanation. "Shiprock poked straight up from the hot center of the earth. Like Devil's Tower in Wyoming."

"You really love this country, don't you?"

"It's home. A place where I fit in."

"And that's what you're looking for. A home."

"Someday I want more family than just Yazzie. Don't you?"

"If anything, I've always had too much family. If you look under *Adams* in the phone book, there's usually ten pages of listing. Dozens of cousins. Mobs of overbearing aunts."

"I was talking about a family of your own. You know, children. A wife. A golden retriever."

"Settling down." He let the words lay there for a moment. "I've given it some thought."

"And?"

"Still thinking."

In Shiprock, they met up with the other agents who fell into line behind them as they proceeded onward toward the tribal meeting place just over the border in Arizona.

The final stretch of road leading to Window Rock zigzagged through rising foothills with thick shrubs. As Dash rounded a curve, he leaned forward and stared. "Son of a bitch," he whispered.

"What is it?"

"A dark green Ford Explorer. That's the car William Graff bought for Russell."

Dash noted the California license plates and the logo from a San Francisco dealership. It had to be Russell. He'd come onto this road knowing that Cara would be headed to the tribal council.

"It can't be," she said. "How can be he driving along like nobody is after him? Russell isn't stupid."

"That's where you're wrong. Criminals—even psychotic madmen—aren't as clever as we give them credit for. That's his car."

Using his cell phone, Dash called the two agents in the following car. "The subject is in the dark green Ford Explorer directly in front of me. I'm going to pass him. Then you close in from behind."

"What should I do?" Cara asked.

"Get in the back and duck down so he won't see you."

While she unfastened her seat belt and went into the rear of the camper, he unholstered his weapon.

"What are you doing?" Cara demanded.

"Pulling my Glock."

"You have no idea how sleazy that sounds."

"For a piece of evidence, you sure are opinionated." She didn't seem the least bit scared. For that, he was glad. "Whatever happens, don't get out of the camper. Understand?"

"Got it."

Though he hadn't intended to use her as bait, that tactic had already proved effective. Until this moment, the manhunt had been futile. No one had seen any sign of Russell. Now he was here. Within sight.

Dash punched the accelerator and edged up beside the Explorer. He wasn't expecting a high-speed chase. There was no reason for Russell to suspect an innocent camper cruising on the paved highway.

Instead of speeding up, the Explorer took an exit. Dash slammed on the brake and swerved right to follow. The camper maneuvered with all the grace of a giant sea turtle. He followed the other vehicle onto a winding two-lane road that pointed toward a low hogback with jagged rocks that looked like the battlements of a medieval castle.

The road was deserted. Why had he gone

this way? They passed a couple of ramshackle little houses, similar to the place where he'd held Cara. Was he leading them to his next victim?

Tension knotted Dash's muscles. His fingers tightened on the steering wheel. He wanted this guy, and he was sick of playing—waiting for the next threatening e-mail, putting up with his father's bitching, trying to understand his warped psychology. He wanted Russell now.

In a burst of speed that pushed the camper's engine to the max, Dash pulled even with the driver's side window and peered through. The man behind the wheel wore sunglasses. A baseball cap shadowed his features. But this had to be Russell.

Dash edged in front of the Explorer. He feathered the brake, gradually slowing down. The Explorer did the same.

"This is weird," Dash said.

"What is?" Cara asked.

"He's not putting up any resistance. He's letting us catch him."

A trap? Some kind of ambush? As soon as the Explorer stopped, trapped between Dash and the other agents, Dash jumped out and dodged behind his car door, using it as a shield. He aimed his gun at the Explorer. He shouted, "FBI. Put your hands where I can see them."

Through the windshield, he saw the driver raise both hands. "Don't shoot," he cried out. "Please don't shoot."

"Keep your hands up."

The other two agents encircled the Explorer. This operation was too simple. Something wasn't right. The Judge had eluded the San Francisco ViCAP force for months. He'd been invisible since he'd kidnapped Cara. Why would he give up so easily now?

Carefully Dash approached the Explorer. He yanked open the driver's side door and stared into the face of a grizzled older man in a stained denim jacket. Not Russell.

"Get out," Dash ordered. "Keep your hands up."

"I ain't done anything wrong," the man whined. "I got the worst damn luck in the world."

When he was cuffed, Dash faced him. "Where did you get this vehicle?"

"It's mine. You can look in the glove compartment, and the title is right there. The kid signed his car over to me. I swear, he did."

"What kid? What's his name?"

"Rusty or something like that. I met him in a diner back in Gallup."

They'd been set up, played for fools. "Why were you on this road?"

"Well, that was part of the deal." The old man licked his lips. "The kid told me I could have this fine vehicle. All's I had to do in return was drive along this stretch of highway for ten miles, then get off at an exit, turn around and drive back the other way."

"Why?"

"Don't know and don't care. I never had a brand-new car in my whole life."

"How long were you supposed to drive back and forth?"

"From ten o'clock until noon." Under the rim of his baseball cap, his dark eyes flickered nervously. He whispered, "That kid. He was looking for somebody."

"Who?"

He nodded toward Dash's vehicle. "Her."

Cara had gotten out of the camper and was coming toward them—casually disregarding his instructions not to leave the vehicle.

Dash turned back to the grizzled idiot. "How do you know it was her?"

"Well, now. He showed me a picture. Said

she was his girlfriend and they had a little spat. You know, a lovers' quarrel."

Dash lifted his gaze to the jagged rock battlements, then looked toward a beat-up shack in the distance. There was a good chance that Russell was nearby, watching them and enjoying his clever little ruse. With a long-range rifle, he could hide in the brush and pick them off one by one.

Quickly, Dash gave orders to the other agents. They should take this moron into custody and turn over the vehicle to forensics for a thorough workup. "Prints, fibers, particles, the whole nine yards."

"Do you think he's in the area?"

"He's probably watching us right now, laughing his damn head off."

"Yes, sir," the agent said. "I'll order a full search with choppers."

"Be sure to clear it through the tribal cops. We're technically on reservation land." He took Cara's arm and pointed her back toward the camper. "I'll take her the rest of the way to Window Rock, and I'll be in touch."

She was rushing to keep up. "What's going on? Who's that guy?"

"I told you to stay in the vehicle."

"But I could see that Russell wasn't here."

"Get in." He slammed his door and started the engine, halfway expecting a bullet through the windshield. As soon as she was inside, he said, "Get in the back and avoid the windows."

"Why?"

"Because Russell could be out there, hiding in the rocks. Because he could have a high-powered rifle aimed at the center of your forehead."

"Good reason." But she wasn't cowed. Though she got in the back, she knelt on the camper floor right behind him. Her face was level with his elbow.

"Hang on," he said. "I want to get away from here fast."

He cranked the steering wheel and sped down the two-lane road toward the highway. The camper wasn't built for speed, but he was moving at a decent clip.

"I guess Russell won this contest," she said.

"You don't need to remind me."

"Like Man Eagle and Son of Light. But there's only one contest that really counts. The last one."

Her rationale didn't make him feel much better.

Russell had proved his point. He knew where Cara would be headed. He was clever enough to call the shots and not get caught.

Dash cursed under his breath.

LYING FLAT ON HIS BELLY atop a mesa, Russell watched through binoculars as the camper driven by the FBI agent whipped down the road toward Window Rock. The big bad federal agent must be feeling pretty stupid, chasing down a wrinkled, old loser who thought he'd gotten a new car.

Something for nothing? There was no such thing. There was always a cost. Scales to be balanced. Judgments to be made.

This time, Russell was the winner. He'd shown them who was in charge. All the stupid cops were forced to dance to his tune.

"What are you doing?" The busty little bleached blonde he'd picked up in Shiprock wriggled up next to him. "What are you looking at?"

"Nothing that concerns you."

"You don't know that, honey."

When she leaned forward to kiss his cheek, he pushed her away. She'd served her purpose, driving the Explorer while he'd followed in his rental car. He had no further need for her. Except as his next victim. Another warning for Cara.

Without a word, he rose and strode back to the car.

"Let's go to Gallup and have some fun." She fluffed her straggly curls. "It's almost noon, and I'm ready for a little drinky-poo."

Her blond hair reminded him of his mother—a comparison that the very upper-class Adele Graff would have despised. His mother owned the best of everything and she flaunted her possessions. Especially him.

From the time he'd been adopted, Russell had been her good little boy, her smart little boy with the curly brown hair. She'd chosen his outfits and dressed him until he was fourteen. She'd undressed him, too.

"Come on," the blonde whined. "I want to have some fun. I want to go dancing."

She did a clumsy shuffle across the mesa top. Her breasts flopped around inside her tight pink T-shirt. A mottled red flush crawled up her throat. Then she stopped, planted her fists on her hips and glared at him. "Come play with me, honey. I know all kinds of games."

He pulled the handgun from the holster clipped to his belt. "Don't move."

She gasped. Her eyes opened wide in surprise.

He took aim. Fired.

The snake that had been only a few feet away from her thick ankles was thrown in the air from the impact of his bullet. It fell lifeless to the dusty rock surface.

The woman whimpered. Pathetic and ugly. There was no need to subject her to testing; he already knew that she was unworthy. "I have no further use for you."

He strode past her to the rental car he intended to exchange immediately for a more anonymous vehicle. The woman clutched his arm. "You saved my life. That was a rattlesnake."

The gun was still in his hand. He pressed the barrel into her soft midsection. "Back off."

She stepped away, finally aware that she might be in danger.

He needed to shoot her, to fill his quota of one victim per day. But guns were ultimately unsatisfying.

He opened the car door and reached into his backpack, finding a pair of handcuffs. He threw them toward her. "Put these on."

"Honey, I don't like this game."

"Do it or I'll shoot off your foot."

Whimpering, she did as he said.

"On your belly," he ordered.

Using a length of rope, he tied her ankles.

"What are you doing?" she cried. "You're not leaving me here?"

Actually, he was. Leaving her behind. Just the way he'd left Adele. But he wanted to make this threat count. Cara had to know he was serious. Drawing his knife, he slashed a careless "X" across her back. Her red blood stained the pink T-shirt.

She screamed.

"Silence. Or I'll cut you again."

Kicking wildly with both feet, she yelled louder.

He flipped her onto her back. He didn't need his knowledge of the human body to know how to make her be quiet. He slashed her throat and stepped back, avoiding the gush of her blood.

In moments, she was still.

He dipped the point of his knife in her blood and scrawled in the sand. One word. *Cara.*

As he drove away, he tossed three eagle feathers out the car window.

There was someone he wanted to talk to. The one person who would tell him he was doing the right thing, that his judgment was correct. But he knew what that voice would say.

He had to do this alone. His own voice was enough. His voice and the sound of his mother crooning at his bedside, stroking his hair off his forehead. He was Mother's good little boy.

Chapter Eleven

Outside the town of Window Rock, Cara moved from the rear of the vehicle into the passenger seat. She could have pointed out the many signs depicting the landmark that had given the town its name—a sandstone arch shaped in a huge circle like a window framing the sky. But she was done playing tour guide.

Russell's elaborate ruse with his car showed that he was willing to risk being caught if it meant getting closer to her. He needed to be stopped. She needed to convince Dash that she should be part of this investigation.

He clicked his cell phone closed. "Before I take you to the council meeting, we need to make a stop at tribal police headquarters. Lieutenant Perry Longhand wants to meet with me."

"I know Perry." A good man. But why did he want to see Dash? "I hope this is more than professional courtesy. A couple of lawmen shaking hands and giving each other steely eyed glares."

"You think I'm steely eyed?"

More like sapphire-blue, but she wasn't about to tell him that his eyes were jewels. That description was much too girlie. "You're very bossy."

"Only when I need to be."

"Not just with me. You snap out orders to other agents and officers. You'd never win the prize for Mr. Congeniality."

"Good," he said. "How do you know Lieutenant Longhand?"

"We've talked about this report I'm presenting at tribal council. It's mostly data on the social problems caused by gambling casinos on reservations. Longhand supports the idea that more funds should be allocated to dealing with increased crime and addictive behavior."

"More money for the police," Dash said. "Of course, he'll support that."

"With increased revenue from the gambling, the tribe can afford it."

She directed him through the dusty little

town of adobe shops, small hogan-style houses and the ubiquitous McDonald's. In seconds, they were at police headquarters.

In Longhand's office, the lieutenant came around his desk and greeted her with a warm hug. Perry was a big, barrel-chested man whose stern features would have been intimidating if he hadn't been so quick to grin.

She smiled back at him. Cara saw him as a brother. On the reservation, a lot of people looked like her. Same broad forehead, same wide jaw, same black hair. When she'd first come here seven years ago, she'd decided to grow her hair long, hoping to be a part of this family.

Longhand pointed out a couple of seats and lowered himself into the swivel chair behind his desk. His office was simple. The desk. A computer. And a window with dusty blinds. One wall was hung with dozens of framed certificates and pictures of his family, including his four children and lovely wife. One of the photographs was an old sepia print of a gray-haired woman in traditional Navajo garb. A grandmother?

Centered on the blotter in front of him was a folder. He toyed with the edges as he spoke. "The chief of police wants me to be your official liaison while the FBI is on the res. We have no problem with your helicopter search, but we want to know before your agents take any sort of action."

"I'll keep you informed," Dash said.

"I read your memo and the APB on this serial killer. The Judge." His eyebrows lowered as he looked toward Cara. "This killer came after you. I'm sorry."

She appreciated his simple offering of sympathy. "I'm all right now."

"He must have been *loco* to attack you." His smile broadened and lit up his dark eyes. "You're a porcupine, Cara. You look playful and innocent. But when somebody crosses you, they're going to get stung."

"You got that right," Dash muttered.

"She giving you a hard time?"

"She refuses to follow simple instructions. Like stay in the car."

Longhand chuckled. "You should have heard her lecture the council about the dangers of casino gambling. I never knew anybody could talk that fast."

"Hey," she interrupted. "I do whatever is necessary."

"And you usually come out on top." As Longhand looked down at the folder, his grin faded. "Now, if you don't mind, Cara. We have police business to discuss. You might want to leave the room. There's coffee in the outer offices and—"

"I'll stay," she said in her authoritative professorial tone. "I might be able to help."

"Police business," he repeated. "About the serial killer."

"I understand."

Longhand looked toward Dash. "Your call, Agent Adams. Does she stay or go?"

Dash studied her, coolly assessing. She matched his gaze with her own determination. If he threw her out, she'd make him sorry.

He gave a quick nod. "She stays."

Perry passed the folder to Dash. "Over a year ago, we found a body. Burned in a fire pit. It could be the work of your serial killer."

Though Dash held the folder so she couldn't see, his expression told her all she needed to know. As he leafed through several photographs, his eyes darkened. His brows arrowed into an angry scowl. "What happened to the body?"

"Buried. It was a long time ago."

"I don't see an autopsy. Or a positive identification. Was there DNA testing?"

"There was jewelry found with her. A ring and a necklace. Silver and onyx. Handmade. They belonged to the daughter of one of our tribal elders—a girl who had gone missing. The elder refused to allow autopsy or any other testing."

Slowly, Dash closed the folder. "Is there any possibility of exhuming the remains?"

She couldn't believe he'd asked that question. Native American burial grounds were sacred. A tribal elder would never allow the FBI to disturb the bones of his daughter.

"You have the crime-scene photos." Longhand's tone was less friendly than a moment ago. "That should be enough."

"Our medical examiners and forensic experts might learn something from her body."

"You have other victims," Longhand said.

"Not from a year ago."

"Why is the timing important?"

"The Judge was active in San Francisco three years ago. He killed seven women, then stopped. The FBI assumed he was dead. Then the killing started again."

"With the woman in Santa Fe," Longhand said. "And the attack on Cara where the killer identified himself."

"Your murder a year ago provides a link

between San Francisco and the present day. If the method is the same, it ties all the crimes more closely to Russell Graff." The timing provided a link to the San Francisco murders. Was it possible that Russell wasn't a copycat, after all? Was he the Judge? "Maybe he never stopped killing."

"Makes sense to me," Longhand said. "But you will never have permission to dig up her body, especially not if you plan to transport her bones to a distant FBI lab. She must be allowed to rest peacefully in her native soil."

Clearly, they were at an impasse. Dash had no jurisdiction in the Navajo nation. He couldn't force an exhumation. Not without creating an incident.

Cara cleared her throat. "I might have a solution."

The two lawmen looked at her as if she were a talking cat—not expected to say anything useful.

"What is it?" Longhand asked.

"There's an archaeological excavation site up toward Mesa Verde—the site where Russell was working. One of the scientists there is a respected forensic anthropologist—Dr. Alexander Sterling. He's working with burial mounds, and he has the sanctioned approval of many tribes."

"I've heard of Dr. Sterling," Longhand said.

"He could be trusted to handle the remains of the murdered woman with the respect they deserve."

Longhand rubbed his hand across his chin, then he slowly nodded. "I'll talk to the father."

"Thank you," Dash said. "If there's any way I can help, don't hesitate to contact me."

Perry Longhand stood behind his desk. "If it's all the same, I'll talk to Cara. She can keep you informed."

She bit her lip to keep from gloating. Whether or not Dash approved, she had become an integral part of this investigation.

IN THE TRIBAL COUNCIL BUILDING, Dash paced the hallway outside the assembly room where business was being discussed. If he'd wanted to be inside, he could have pressured someone to let him observe even though everyone on the reservation seemed to take great pleasure in reminding him that the FBI had no jurisdiction here. But he couldn't care less about politics. Not for the Navajo or for anybody else.

Politics and law represented the life he'd rejected long ago. Cara had called him a hunter, and he was itching to get back to the chase. During the last two hours, a lot had happened.

The tribal elder had given his permission to allow Dr. Sterling to exhume and examine his daughter's remains. Sterling had agreed and was on his way here.

Dash had arranged for the pertinent autopsy documents to be faxed to Lieutenant Longhand's office so Sterling could compare them to his findings.

A helicopter search of the reservation was underway along the highway corridor. The results so far: zippo.

And, somehow, Cara had gone from being a protected witness to joining the investigative team. Whether or not he approved, there were things she could do that no one else could. Her suggestion to use Dr. Sterling for the autopsy was brilliant.

His cell phone rang, and he stepped outside to take the call. It was one of the field agents on the helicopter search. "We found something. A young woman."

Silently, Dash prayed. *Not another victim.* "Is she dead?"

"Yes. A blonde. She was out here in the middle of nowhere. Handcuffed. Her ankles were tied. Her throat slashed."

Dash continued his pacing outside. He went along the sidewalk leading to the parking lot outside the council building and back again.

Bitter disappointment rose in the back of his throat. "Anything else?"

"Russell had a message."

Dash was pretty damned sure he didn't want to hear it. Still, he said, "Give it to me."

"Until he has what he wants, others will die."

Of course. "Keep me posted on new developments."

Dash disconnected the call with a snap. He hated the way Russell was toying with him. This twenty-four-year-old punk was playing a sick poker game where he held all the good cards. Except for one. Dash had the ace in the hole. Cara.

She'd volunteered to be used as bait, and at this point he was almost ready to take her up on the offer. It was doubtful that the FBI would give official approval for that kind of action, but he'd gone against procedure before. As Flynn had pointed out, Dash had a reputation for risk-aggressive behavior.

If he set up a sting, she'd agree to do it. Her motivation came from Russell's current strategy of "punishing one person a day" and blaming it on her. She wasn't the sort to accept that. Cara was strong, and she had more self-control than a Zen master. She was brave enough. After that one long night when she'd sobbed in his arms, she hadn't shown much fear.

But she'd also told him her dreams. She wanted a home and family. She wanted to belong with someone. If he could give it to her, if he could be that someone…

Instead, he was planning to use her.

Standing in the parking lot outside the building where the tribal delegates had gathered, he noticed a sharp disparity. Among the mostly beat-up older cars were a couple of big, shiny new Cadillacs—an indication that the casino revenues had begun to kick in.

His gaze lifted to the hazy blue skies that hung above dull red hills. Even the green of springtime seemed muted. As the afternoon sun slipped lower, shadows stretched out from the mesas, carving layers of texture from the hills and rocks. If he stared long enough, this land—Cara's land—wasn't plain and ugly. It wasn't pretty, but it was…

He watched another car pull into the parking lot. A new one. Probably a rental. This could be the famous Dr. Alexander Sterling, but he doubted it. The anthropologist was coming from a dig site; he probably drove something more rugged.

The sedan parked. The door opened. William Graff strode toward him. What the hell was he doing here?

Dressed in a long-sleeved black sweater and gray trousers, Russell's father looked sophisticated and urban, more at home on a golf course than the Navajo reservation. His face pulled into a deep frown like a mask of tragedy.

Dash braced himself, ready for a fight. Almost eager, in fact. He hated Graff for the way he'd disrespected Cara, suggesting that she'd seduced his son. For a moment, he considered greeting the elder Graff with a left jab to the face, hard enough to break that long, thin nose.

"Agent Adams," Graff snapped. "I understand my son's car has been located."

"That's correct."

"Can I have the vehicle released to me?"

"No." Dash was blunt.

"On the drive here, I saw helicopters. Are you chasing him down with choppers?"

I wish. "Russell has not been taken into custody."

When Graff removed his sunglasses, his dark eyes were underlined with exhaustion. "I've come here to offer my assistance in your investigation."

Dash doubted that his motives were innocent. "What do you want in return?"

"Russell needs help. Both his mother and I agree. Our boy is troubled. He needs a psychiatric evaluation."

Dash recognized the ploy. William Graff was trying to set up an insanity plea for his serial-killer son, trying to get Russell off with a few years of counseling in a posh psychiatric facility. "How can you help me find your son?"

"In the past two days, he has made substantial cash withdrawals from an account set up to pay for his education. The total amount is nearly forty thousand dollars."

"I thought we had all of Russell's financial information." Following the money was one of the best ways to track a fugitive. "Did you purposely withhold this information?"

"I didn't know. This account is administered by his mother. She told me about the withdrawal this morning."

"Your wife could be charged with aiding and abetting."

Graff's frown deepened. "I didn't have to tell you about this. I'm cooperating. She's cooperating."

And trying to save his own ass. Dash turned away from him and pulled his cell phone from his pocket. "As of now, all your accounts are frozen pending further investigation."

"You can't do that."

"The hell I can't." The damage had already been done. Russell had enough cash that he didn't need to use his bank withdrawal cards or credit cards. That doorway for tracking his movements had slammed shut.

"Listen to me," Graff demanded. "I'm trying to help."

"All you've done thus far is obstruct a federal investigation. You're not above the law, Mr. Graff. Nor is your wife. And especially not your son."

Graff sneered as he replaced his sunglasses on the bridge of his thin nose. "I'll tell you this much. My son might be crazy, but he's not wrong."

"About what?"

"You call him the Judge. Because he passes out judgment, and he's right to do so. Some people aren't worthy. They don't deserve to live."

Dash opened his eyes and really looked at William Graff. He remembered Cara's impression that someone else had been with Russell when he'd held her captive. "What about you, Mr. Graff? Are you a judge?"

"Every day of my life I have to make judgments. Deciding who to trust, who to hire, who to fire."

"That's not what I'm asking." And he knew it. "Tell me about the women in your life."

"I have never been unfaithful to my wife, Adele."

"Never found any other woman worthy?"

William Graff pivoted on his heel and walked away, leaving Dash with unanswered questions. Had Graff come here to set up his son's insanity plea? Was he trying to protect himself and his wife? Or was he taunting Dash?

William Graff was a bully. That much Dash knew for sure. And his adopted son, Russell, must have struggled to fulfill his father's expectations—a goal he would inevitably fail to achieve. Possible motive, for Russell. Unless they were working together. Father and son serial killers.

Chapter Twelve

Flush with excitement after the presentation of her report at the tribal council, Cara had actually forgotten about the investigation for a few minutes. As soon as she got into the car with Dash, that respite was over. They were on their way to the Indian Hospital in nearby Fort Defiance where Dr. Sterling was using the morgue to process the exhumed remains of the murdered girl.

This time, Cara hoped to avoid seeing the body. She didn't need another reminder of Russell's brutality. Nor did she want to ask the question that had been simmering in the back of her mind all day. *Was there another victim?*

By the time they reached the hospital parking lot, she couldn't put it off any longer. She adjusted her captain's chair until she was facing Dash. It was almost dark, but he'd parked under a light. She could see him clearly. "It's been almost another full day," she said. "Has he punished anyone else?"

"A woman," he said. "A blonde."

"God, no." Horror pulsed through her. The drumbeat of the dead. She didn't want to know what had happened to this blonde, but she couldn't hide from the terrible truth.

"I'm sorry, Cara." He swiveled his captain's chair toward her. Their knees were almost touching.

"Is she…"

"Dead. Her throat was slashed."

"That doesn't sound like Russell." She shook her head in desperate denial. "And the woman was blond. He always attacks brunettes. Maybe this murder is unrelated."

"I'm afraid not," he said. "Your name was written in the dirt beside the body."

Another murder placed at her doorstep. Her hands covered her face, hiding from the sudden wash of guilt. This blond woman had died because of Cara. She was responsible. Russell had promised to continue his reign of terror until he had her.

If she truly believed that her own death would end this madness, she might have offered herself as the next victim. Would that stop him? Would that end the madness?

As she lowered her hands, her fingers clenched. There was no guarantee that her own sacrifice would cause Russell to change. He was a stone-cold murderer.

Anger cut through her guilt and her sorrow for the blond victim. "We have to find him, Dash. To stop him."

"I know." He reached over and placed his hand on her thigh. A gesture of comfort? Or something else? "We will stop him."

"But how? His behavior is all over the place. He's shooting cops. Murdering women who don't fit the profile."

"There's only one consistent part," Dash said. "You."

"I'll do anything to help the investigation," she said. "You understand that, don't you?"

"It's my job to keep you safe."

When she looked into his eyes, she saw something more than a Fed doing his job. He cared about her on a deeper level. In spite of everything—her guilt, her horror and her rage—her heart jumped inside her rib cage. She couldn't help responding to this attraction.

Why couldn't this be happening in a different time? In a different place?

"Damn it, I want to go back to the way my life was before Russell. Calm. Predictable. And blessedly boring."

"I doubt it was all that dull."

"You don't know me, Dash. My idea of high excitement is a Vivaldi CD, a double shot of espresso and a good book."

"Sounds pretty exciting to me."

"You're a firecracker with a lit fuse. I can't imagine you sitting still to read a book."

"I like to read naked." His hand inched up her thigh. His fingers exerted a subtle pressure. "We'd be side by side on the bed. I'd turn the pages for you. One by one."

She swallowed with a gulp, realizing that they weren't at the safe house anymore. No surveillance. No one was watching. "I can turn pages by myself, thank you."

"It's more fun my way."

"Nude?"

"That's right. And we could act out the scenes. The sexy parts."

"What happened to you while I was in that meeting?" She could feel her heartbeat accelerate. "A few hours ago, you were all business. Mr. Fed. Now you're…Casanova."

"You're right. I shouldn't be talking like this."

But when he lifted his hand from her leg, she caught his wrist and firmly guided his palm back to her thigh. With her other hand, she reached up and touched his cheek. His incredibly blue eyes glowed, hot and penetrating. Meeting his gaze, she whispered, "I like Casanova."

"I like you, Cara. And I hate that you're in danger. After we talk to Dr. Sterling, I'm taking you back to the safe house."

She didn't want to go back. "You need me, Dash. Russell won't come out of hiding unless he thinks he's getting close to me."

"I'm the only one who gets to be close to you."

His next move was so fast that she didn't quite comprehend what was happening. His free hand tangled in her hair. He pulled her face toward his. His mouth joined with hers in a hard, demanding kiss. Unexpected. Startling.

At the same time, this was exactly what she wanted and needed. Years of sensible repression fell away as her tongue slid through her lips. Hungrily, she welcomed him. His taste. His scent. She wanted everything he could give her.

She scooted to the edge of her chair, needing to be closer to him. Her knees were trapped between his spread thighs in a strangely erotic position. She directed his hand inside her suit jacket to her breast. He squeezed. His thumb flicked her nipple. Wild sensations unfurled inside her. More. She wanted more.

But he broke away from her and swiveled his chair so he was facing forward, staring through the windshield. "I shouldn't have done that."

"Wrong." She was gasping. "You made exactly the right move."

He whispered a low curse. "Following my instincts could put you in danger."

She had a bad feeling. "We're not talking about sex, are we?"

"I want you, Cara. That goes without saying."

But she wouldn't mind hearing it, listening to him tell her that she was desirable and fantastic. "What are you talking about?"

He lightly smacked the steering wheel with the heel of his hand. "I can't believe I'm even considering this plan."

"What plan?"

"Using you as bait."

This time when he looked at her she saw concern and doubt instead of desire. "Dash,

I'll do *anything* to help. *Anything.* I can't stand thinking that Russell is still hurting people because of me."

"His actions aren't your fault."

"I know, but it feels like…" Both hands flew to her breast, holding in the pain of regret that mounted with every victim. The burned remains in Mesa Verde. The deputy who was shot. The woman who was tied up. "Use me any way that you need to."

"We should go into the hospital now," he said. "Russell was seen on the reservation, so we need to be on high alert. I'm your bodyguard, and I want you to pay attention."

He was back in control. Mr. Fed in his sports coat. She much preferred Casanova. "Fine."

"You need to do exactly what I say. No questions. No second-guessing. Just action. If I say hit the ground, you do it. If I say run, you sprint."

"And if you say kiss me, should I jump on you and rip open your shirt?"

"This isn't a joke, Cara."

"I'm not laughing." She shoved open her door.

"Stop." He caught hold of her arm before she could get out. "I'll open the door for you after I've made sure you're not stepping into Russell's waiting arms."

She sank back into her seat. This bodyguard business wasn't going to be any fun at all.

As they walked to the hospital entrance, Dash rested his hand on the small of her back. When she looked up at him, she noticed the small movements of his head. His eyes were in constant motion, scanning for danger.

Even as they were escorted through the corridor of the two-story hospital, he kept watch. In the basement level, far from the normal hospital activity, they found Lieutenant Perry Longhand leaning against the wall with his arms folded across his broad chest. His face was serious as he greeted them.

"Dr. Sterling is in there." Longhand nodded toward a pair of swinging doors, wide enough for a gurney. Though the doors weren't labeled, Cara assumed this was the morgue.

Nervously, she toyed with the turquoise beads around her throat. "How is the elder's family?"

"Troubled. They'll do a Blessingway ceremony tonight." He pushed open the door to the morgue. "I'll tell Dr. Sterling you're here."

When she glanced over her shoulder at Dash, she caught a glimpse of his former passion. Good. He hadn't completely turned into RoboCop.

The door from the morgue swung open, and Dr. Sterling came through. He wore a protective gown over his shirt, jeans and boots. While working with the body, he would have been wearing protective gloves, but he'd already removed them. He clasped her hand. His hazel eyes confronted her with a disconcerting directness. "I'm pleased to see you again, Cara."

"Thank you for agreeing to this examination."

"I was rather pleased to be summoned away from the dig site. Dr. Petty seems to have lost control of his students with this news. They're moping all day and chattering all night about Russell Graff."

She could easily imagine. The teams working at archaeological sites often took on the characteristics of bickering siblings. "And what is your opinion of Russell?"

"A very good student." He released her hand. "That young man knows how to follow instructions, and he has the patience of a true scientist."

This was a high compliment from Dr. Sterling, whose conclusions were always meticulous and detailed. He was, possibly, the most intelligent person she'd ever known.

She guessed that his age was somewhere in his forties, but it was hard to tell. His face was unlined, a result of seldom revealing emotion with either a smile or a frown. His hair was thinning on top, making his forehead seem too large. A big head for a big brain.

When Dash stepped up beside him, the contrast between the two men was obvious. Dash—a man of action—was lean and quick, bursting with vital energy. Beside him, Dr. Sterling appeared almost bloodless.

Dash introduced himself, shook hands and got right to the point. "Have you reached any conclusion about these remains?"

"Several," he said.

Cara suggested, "Perhaps we could go upstairs to the cafeteria and get a cup of coffee."

Dr. Sterling glanced back toward the swinging doors. "I can't leave her alone."

"I'll stay," Longhand volunteered. "Bring me back an orange soda."

THOUGH THE HOSPITAL CAFETERIA offered the usual selection of chips and sandwiches, Dash chose a fried bread taco and another dish that looked like hominy. Cara called it *posole*. He avoided the watery-looking coffee.

At a rectangular table, he sat beside Cara with his back to the wall so he could observe the entrances and exits. Sterling sat opposite them.

Cara had also loaded her tray with food. Lamb stew and fried bread.

Sterling had only a mug of tea without sugar. His manner was austere, as if he couldn't be bothered with such mundane things as food. He opened the folder of material that Dash had arranged to be faxed—prior autopsies on the Judge's victims. Sterling slipped on a pair of reading glasses and skimmed through the pages.

Dash asked, "Is there any possibility of DNA testing on these remains?"

"I found tissue, highly degraded but viable. However, I can't allow any part of that young woman to be separated from her remains. I promised her parents that she would be returned intact to her grave."

"Don't you think they'd want to know for certain that the victim is their daughter?"

"I concur with the prior identification," he said. "Her skull structure is typical of the Pueblo tribes. Her height is correct. At one time, she had a broken arm that matches the records from this very hospital. Besides which, her parents seem satisfied that this is their child. That's the most salient factor."

Dash tasted the posole. An interesting combination of peppers and spices mingled with corn. "Have you reached any preliminary conclusions on the comparison with other cases?"

"Normally, I prefer waiting until my examination is complete, but I understand your urgency."

Again, Sterling studied the notes and photographs. His silence was irritating, but Dash had no choice but to wait.

If Sterling verified that this killing could be attributed to the Judge, it created a pattern that pointed more directly to Russell. The timing of this murder suggested that he'd never stopped, that he was the same man who'd murdered seven women in San Francisco. Not a copycat.

Russell had a ritual and he followed it. Until Cara.

Dash glanced toward her as she dipped her fried bread into the stew and took a bite.

She looked back at him and winked. Behind her supposedly innocent smile, he saw a teasing glimmer of sensuality—a reminder of the passion that had overwhelmed him in the parking lot. What the hell had he been thinking? The answer to that question was pretty damned obvious. He wanted her.

He'd been constantly in her presence since the moment he'd rescued her from that field beside the flaming house. He'd watched her transformation from a terrified creature to a self-assured, powerful woman. A sexually confident woman.

His gaze fell on the turquoise beads that rested at the delicate hollow below her throat. Her skin was so smooth and fine.

"I've noticed several common elements," Sterling said. "My preliminary opinion is that the woman in the morgue was almost certainly a victim of the San Francisco killer. The Judge."

"What about the victim found recently in Santa Fe and the other at Mesa Verde?"

"There's some deviation."

"Such as?"

"I'll need further microscopic analysis to be certain, but in the earlier murders there appears to be more damage to the bone. Indications of severe incisions and even fractures."

Dash wasn't following Dr. Sterling's analysis. "What does that mean?"

"In the earlier murders, he spent more time playing with the bodies postmortem."

This was an aspect of the crime that Dash had read in the reports but hadn't focused on. "Playing?"

"After his victims were dead, the killer performed clumsy dissections. Cutting away pieces of flesh and organs. Possibly to make incineration more efficient." Sterling's gaze was unwavering. "There's less postmortem damage in the more recent victims."

Dash set his fork on the tray, glad that he wasn't eating meat. "But it's the same killer, right?"

"Possibly." Sterling raised his mug to his lips and glanced over the rim at Cara. "What does this variance suggest to you, Dr. Messinger?"

"He's lost interest in cutting." She shook her head. "But that doesn't seem right. According to the profilers, serial killers are supposed to escalate their behavior."

"I'm a scientist." Sterling's voice held a note of disdain. "Not a psychologist."

"Possibly," Cara said, "there's less skeletal damage because he's gotten better at what he's doing."

"That would be my hypothesis," Sterling said. "If, in fact, Russell is your killer, his postmortem dissection technique has improved. He's neater, with less gouging. If it is Russell...in my working with this young man, I have noticed a marked improvement in his abilities."

"Do you believe Russell is the killer?" Dash asked.

"I draw no final conclusions." A thin smile touched his lips. "That's your job, Agent Adams."

As if he needed reminding.

Sterling turned toward Cara again. "I had a message for you from Joanne Jones."

"Russell's girlfriend?"

"I couldn't say. I have better things to do than keep up with the many romances at the dig site."

"The message?" Cara asked.

"She wanted me to say hello and to

mention that she was looking forward to seeing you at the dig site. And there was something else. She was very specific about these words. I should tell you that she would 'catch you later.'"

Catch you later. The words Russell used to sign his e-mails to Cara. It was no coincidence that his girlfriend had used that phrase while inviting Cara to the dig site.

Dash had to go there, had to follow up on this clue. More importantly, he had to take Cara with him.

Chapter Thirteen

Waiting inside the camper, Cara fidgeted in the passenger seat. Dash's new plan to keep her protected was to lock her up in here like a bird in a cage, a sardine in a can. Through the windshield, she glared at him as he talked to two other agents.

They were parked at the far edge of a motel lot, and she had no idea what Dash was discussing with his Fed buddies. Were they going to stay here for the night? Were they going somewhere more secure? Nobody told her anything.

She watched as Dash gestured emphatically. Even in springtime, the night air was chilly, and he was wearing his black leather jacket with the collar turned up. He looked a little dangerous, as if he'd finally been pushed too far.

She exhaled a frustrated sigh. As long as she was stuck here waiting, she might as well get something done. Swiveling around in her captain's chair, she faced the rear of the camper. The small enclosed space had a kitchenette on one side and a narrow bench that could double as a bed on the other. She found her briefcase and returned to her chair.

A table folded out in front of her. After turning on the overhead light, she opened the briefcase and took out the last few term papers she had left to grade—freshmen papers on basic, boring topics. With a red pen, she slashed aggressively at minor errors. Then, to compensate for her bad mood, she gave higher grades than these students deserved.

Turning, she glanced through the windshield. Dash was still talking. Still ignoring her. It might be nice to know where she stood with him. That kiss they'd shared before going into the hospital told her that she was more than a protected witness. How much more? Would there be more intimacy? For a man of action, he was certainly taking his time when it came to her. She lowered her pen and ripped through a misspelled word. Couldn't anyone get it right?

She flipped to the next paper, unfastened the clip and started to read about Anasazi pottery shards. No earth-shattering revelations here. Same old stuff.

The second page was different. Only a few printer-generated lines were centered on the white paper.

"Cara," it said. "You left me in haste. Too soon to realize that we are meant to be together. No other mate is worthy. Come to me, Cara. At the place of long shadows, I will find you and put an end to my quest. The Judge."

How had Russell slipped this message into her stack of term papers? When? He must have gone into her office at the university. He knew her too well, knew that she would demand to have her papers to grade. No matter where she went or what she did, he was always there. Inescapable.

This new threat sent her pulse racing. She wanted to run, to scream, to throw a tantrum. But she wasn't a child. She needed to make an intelligent, measured decision.

His reference to the place of long shadows couldn't have been more direct. At the archaeological dig site where Russell, Joanne and Dr. Sterling worked was a pictograph carved into stone—stick figures of dancers followed by their shadows. Long shadows.

Russell awaited her there.

The driver's side door opened, and Dash climbed inside. He had a couple of plastic grocery bags, which he stowed behind his captain's chair.

"About time," she said.

"Nice to see you, too."

Without another word, she shoved Russell's message toward him. "I found this tucked inside the papers I was grading."

He read aloud, "The place of long shadows?"

"A reference to the archaeology site where Russell was working." Her decision was made. Firmly, she said, "We have to go there. Both of us. You and me. Together."

"I agree."

His ready acceptance shocked her. She narrowed her eyes, trying to see inside his mind. His objections to including her in the investigation had been unwavering. "Why are you being so agreeable?"

"Turn that chair around and buckle up," he said. "We're on our way."

As they pulled out of the parking lot, she asked, "Are we going directly to the dig site?"

"We'll spend the night at Pilar Canyon. According to those agents I was talking to, those campsites have good access and visibility."

The fact that he had their route all mapped told her that he'd made this plan earlier. "When did you decide this?"

"When we were talking to Dr. Sterling."

She frowned. "Surely you don't suspect him of anything."

"I suspect everybody," Dash said.

"Sterling is a genius."

"And a little warped. How many people have advanced degrees in the study of dead bodies?"

"Very few. And forensic anthropology is a whole lot more than bones. Some of Dr. Sterling's findings have changed the way we understand ancient societies."

"Don't worry. I'm not seriously interested in him as a suspect." His gaze flicked to the rearview mirrors, still keeping watch. "But I can't say the same for the other students at the dig site. Russell's buddies might have been in contact with him."

"Especially Joanne Jones," she said. "Do you think Russell is there?"

"It makes sense for him to return to a place where he knows the lay of the land. It's a comfort zone."

She still wasn't satisfied with his explanation. "Why did you decide to take me along?"

"Don't get me wrong, Cara. As soon as we're done at the dig site, I'm taking you back to the safe house."

That still wasn't an answer. "Again, why?"

He turned toward her. In the light from the dashboard, she saw him smile. "Because I need your help."

Exactly what she wanted to hear. *He needed her.* A giddy sense of adventure welled up inside her. They were going after a serial killer. Serious business. Still, she couldn't keep from grinning.

"Man Eagle," she said.

"The Hopi legend about the serial killer." His expression turned skeptical. "Listen, Cara. I know Russell has been leaving behind his weird little clues. The bowl, the ceremonial pipe and eagle feather."

"What about that bowl?" she asked. "Did it belong to Russell?"

He nodded. "We found his thumbprint. But don't ask me why he left it there. It doesn't make sense. This isn't a neat little story that can be tied up in a folk table."

"I can't explain Russell," she said, "but I

have a pretty good idea about you and me. When you first heard the story of Man Eagle, you asked if it had a moral."

"And you said no."

"Actually, there is a lesson in the story. Son of Light never would have defeated Man Eagle without asking for help from others. You need me."

"More than you know."

She sat back in her seat and savored this lovely, warm feeling. More than just a witness, she was needed. Necessary. They were a team.

Though it was only a bit after nine o'clock, there were few other cars on this straight, two-lane road. She could see headlights approaching from miles away.

Dash fiddled with the various dials and screens on the dashboard, programming the air flow and the GPS mapping function. He turned up the sound, and the smooth voice of Harry Connick Jr. gently serenaded her.

She recalled Dash's earlier discussion with Flynn about musical taste. "You're not a country-western guy."

"Not usually."

"Is this your CD?"

"It's an iPod mix. I take it on trips for when I jog. Mostly jazz."

It wasn't hard for her to imagine him in a dimly lit jazz club in San Francisco. His normal life was so far away from the Southwest. Far away from her. "Do you miss San Francisco?"

"Not really. San Francisco happens to be where I'm living right now, but I haven't put down roots."

He wasn't ready to settle down. She knew that about him. Dash was a rolling stone who had already left a law career and a wife. "What are you looking for?"

"A good laugh, a soft bed and a great cup of coffee."

Life wasn't that simple, and neither was he. She'd caught glimpses of a complicated man. Strong and sensitive. He was interested in new knowledge and information, but when he made up his mind, the decision was as solid as granite.

And he'd decided that he needed her. Tonight they would be alone. Just the two of them, alone in their camper mini-home.

No wonder she was excited. Peeking over her shoulder, she checked out the very narrow bed that hugged the wall of the camper. It didn't look big enough for one skinny person. "Where are we going to sleep?"

"That bench folds out into a full bed. And there's another bed in the back. We don't have to, um, you know."

This was the first time she'd heard him sound unsure of himself. "We don't have to sleep together?"

"Right."

She reached across the space between the two captain's chairs and stroked the cool leather of his jacket. "One bed will be enough."

As he turned toward her, the nose of the camper swerved. The music on the mix switched to classic Isaac Hayes with a hard, pounding beat. "I don't want to pressure you, Cara."

"And you don't want me to get the wrong idea," she said. "I understand."

"Do you?"

She had a very clear picture of Dashiell Quincy Adams. "A federal agent who has already been married once. There's no room in your life for a relationship, and you have no intention of settling down again."

"That's an accurate profile."

Though she might want more from him, Cara knew what to expect. Her eyes were wide open. Tonight, she would make love to him. And that would have to be enough.

THE TOPOGRAPHY OF PILAR CANYON met Dash's requirement for a safe site. It was desolate. No one had followed them. For the past ten miles, he hadn't seen another vehicle.

At the unmanned camping area, he'd parked on a high ridge overlooking a pine forest. Even if, by some freak chance, Russell located the camper, he couldn't approach without making noise.

While Dash fumbled in the back of the camper, flipping down panels to make a bigger bed, Cara had stepped outside to catch a breath of air. She'd promised to stay close.

Soon, they'd be even closer.

When he climbed out of the camper, he saw her standing at the edge of the rock overlooking a deep canyon. Her chin tilted upward, and her face was bathed in moonlight. The dry winds played with her long black hair.

As he came up behind her, she didn't turn. His arms glided around her slender body, and he pulled her close. She smelled like flowers and fresh mint.

"What do you think of me?" she asked.

"You're beautiful."

He nuzzled through the curtain of hair to

kiss the warm nape of her neck, and she released a tiny but very sexy sigh. "Really, Dash. I told you my opinions. Now you tell me."

"You want a profile?"

She wiggled her butt against him, and his groin tightened. He was already primed for lovemaking. In the back of his mind, he'd been thinking about sex for days.

"A profile." Her voice was husky. "That's exactly what I want."

"Determined. Ambitious. Intelligent. Maybe a little too smart for your own good because you tend to overthink." She shifted against him, and the friction of their bodies aroused him even more. "You take your Navajo heritage seriously. When I saw you standing here in the moonlight, you seemed like part of this land."

"But I'm really not. As much as I appreciate the time I spend at the reservation, I always feel like an observer. I don't speak the language. I don't even know how to ride a horse."

"You're a city girl."

"An overly educated city girl. When you requested DNA testing on the murdered daughter of the elder, I found myself agreeing with you. Tribal rites are important, but I wanted justice for that victim. For all the victims found on sacred sites and in burial mounds."

He didn't want to get her started talking about archaeology. "Are you nervous?"

"Maybe," she admitted.

He could go slow. After one last kiss on her neck, he separated from her. Standing at her side, he peered into the depths of the rugged canyon. He repeated the question she'd asked him earlier. "What are you looking for?"

"A place where I belong. It's not really the reservation. Or in my career where there's so much competition. I never fit in with my very blond family."

"Right now," he said, "you belong with me."

Her lips parted in a smile. "That's so simple."

"Life doesn't have to be complex."

Her hands slipped inside his jacket and she pulled him toward her. When they kissed, the canyon winds swirled around them—a cool contrast to the moist heat of her mouth. Her soft female body molded against him.

The kiss ended; they were both gasping.

She grabbed his hand and pulled him toward the camper. "Come on, Dash. Hurry."

"We've got all night."

"I want you now." Cara was so eager that she tripped over her own feet on the way to the camper. Inside, she was delighted to see that the entire back section had been turned into a bed.

Quickly, she shed her coat and stretched out on top of the blankets covering the mattress. Not exactly a feather bed, but fairly comfortable. If she stretched her arm out to the right, she could touch the faucets in the mini-sink.

As Dash peeled off his leather jacket, he bumped his head against the ceiling. "Not much room in here."

"It's like a cocoon," she said.

He locked the doors and started the music again.

"Won't that run down the battery?"

"Separate adapter," he said. "No juice from the car."

A cool instrumental jazz piece softly teased her senses. She watched as he slipped out of his shoulder holster and stretched out on the bed. He kept his handgun within easy reach—a reminder of all the dangers that lay outside their camper cocoon.

She snuggled into his embrace. Their lips joined, setting off a chain reaction of sensation. A fiery heat raced through her body. She belonged here. With him. For tonight, this was home.

In the glow of moonlight through the rear window, she gazed into his eyes. From the first time she'd seen him, those deep-set blue eyes had drawn her toward this moment in his arms.

Holding her gaze, his fingers expertly unbuttoned her blouse, exposing her black lace bra. He unfastened the front hook, freeing her breasts.

"Smooth move," she said. "How did you learn to do that?"

"FBI."

When she laughed, he lowered his head to kiss her throat and then her breasts. With aching tenderness, he suckled her taut nipples, and the fire inside her grew.

With his skillful fingers, he undid the button on her slacks and parted the zipper. His hand glided over her panties. She parted her thighs, welcoming his touch.

Her muscles tensed and released. Desire throbbed in every cell of her body. The sweet jazz music harmonized with a sexy internal rhythm. Pure sensation.

She was ready for sex yet she wanted to savor the moment, to make it last.

"Dash," she whispered.

"What is it?"

"Your shirt. It needs to come off."

He lay beside her, his head propped up on an elbow, waiting for her to remove his shirt. But she wasn't as clever as he was. Her fingers plucked clumsily at the buttons. Damn it, this was taking too long. She gathered the material in each hand, but before she could rip it apart, he stopped her.

"Let me take it off," he said.

"All off," she demanded.

She wanted to see the muscular, lean body that had tantalized her for days. And she wasn't disappointed. Broad, well-muscled shoulders. Narrow torso. His chest hair was an enticing, dark pelt that arrowed into the waistband of his jeans.

There wasn't enough space in the back of the camper for a striptease. Dash pulled off his shoes, socks and jeans with more efficiency than sexiness, but the end result was spectacular.

He pounced on her. "If you think you're going to be dressed while I'm naked, forget it."

At the foot of the bed, he removed her

sneakers and socks. His thumb pressed into the arch of her foot. Being careful with the cuts and bruises that had just healed, he massaged the sole of her foot and her toes. His touch sent a current of electricity up her legs to the core of her sensuality, setting off delightful shivers of pure desire.

He slid her slacks down her legs. Removed her blouse and bra. She was naked except for the turquoise beads at her throat and the silver cuffs on her wrists.

He laced his fingers with hers and pulled until she was sitting on the bed, facing him. For a long moment, they merely stared, each of them drinking in the other.

When she looked into his face, he smiled and she saw a dimple she'd never noticed before.

He opened his arms to her, and she moved gently into his embrace. Her hand gracefully traced the line of his torso. There was a synchronized elegance to the way they moved together. Like dancers. They were meant to be together. A perfect fit.

She wanted to know every part of his body. Intimately. Trailing her fingers through his chest hair and down his torso, she grasped his hard, hot erection.

He tensed. "Careful. I want to take my time."

But she was ready to take their passion to the next level. "Condom?"

"Yes." He kissed her.

After he sheathed himself, he lowered her to the bed. The weight of his body pressed on top of her, and she arched her back, wanting to be closer to him, wanting him inside her.

Where had he been all her life? She'd always enjoyed sex, but never like this. With him, she was transcendent, ethereal. This blue-eyed man was taking her to a place she'd never been.

A saxophone wailed on the soundtrack. Her dance had become more demanding. A fierce tango. She shimmied against him, pulled him so tightly against her that their flesh melted together. And still, he held back.

She rolled on top of him, but he flipped her back. And he entered her with a long, slow thrust. She whimpered, "More. Faster."

He moved inside her. "You feel so good."

Her pulse fluttered. An intense energy was building inside her, driving her wild. She heard herself moaning, gasping. Her muscles constricted in a fierce spasm that demanded release. As he thrust harder and faster, her world shattered in a prolonged explosion.

His body quaked above her.

Fireworks.

Passion.

Then, they both were still. Suspended in ecstasy. She exhaled a long satisfied sigh as delicious shivers rose from her core and raced across her skin. If making love was something Dash had learned in the FBI, she'd never again date anyone but Feds.

Chapter Fourteen

The next morning, Dash climbed out of the camper at a few minutes past seven o'clock. Shirtless, he stretched and yawned. It was a beautiful spring day, drenched in sunlight. The subtle hues of the granite cliffs and scruffy pines reminded him of an artist's painting. This rugged landscape wasn't so dull, after all.

Cara tumbled out beside him. With her hair tousled and her shirt half-buttoned, she didn't look anything like a learned archaeology professor. She was amazing. Her lips were curved in the goofy smile of a woman who had been well loved. Three times.

She spread her arms in a salute to the sun. "I feel like a butterfly coming out of her cocoon."

"Don't fly too far." He reached into the camper, grabbed his leather jacket and slipped it on. "I'd like to get to the dig site before they're busy. What time does the work get underway?"

"The schedule is pretty relaxed, depending on the weather."

When she met his gaze, her grin took on a more subtle shading. He knew there was something on her mind. Being able to read her expressions pleased him. She was like a well-crafted book with a twist on every page. "What is it, Cara?"

"About last night…"

"What about it? Are you going to give me a grade?"

"Is there anything higher than A-plus?"

"You could give me extra credit."

He reached toward her, but she moved away. Though she seemed to be glowing, her eyes were serious. "I want you to know that I'm not one of *those* women. Just because we had amazing sex, it doesn't mean you owe me something."

He hadn't been thinking about their relationship, hadn't been thinking at all.

She continued, "I don't expect gifts or flowers or any kind of commitment."

Her frank assessment bothered him. The way she described last night sounded a lot like a one-night stand, and he didn't see her that way. She was incredible. A once-in-a-lifetime woman. "What if I said I wanted a commitment?"

"I wouldn't believe you. You're an FBI field agent who loves his job. You're married to your work—your often dangerous work—and there isn't room for much else in your life."

Which was one of the reasons his first marriage had ended in divorce. "I could make some room. Rearrange the furniture."

"That's not what I'm looking for." Her gaze turned inward. "I'm in my thirties. After what happened with Russell, I realized that I'm not going to live forever."

"That's not an uncommon reaction. I've seen it before in victims." When facing their own mortality, people looked at their life in a different way. "You're thinking of all the things you haven't done, the sights you haven't seen, the experiences you might have missed out on."

"Yes," she said.

"Maybe you want to jump out of an airplane. Or go backpacking in Tibet."

"I want a family. A home." She glided into his arms. "I want to settle down and that's something I would never ask of you."

Her body was so soft, so warm and pliant. He wanted to make love to her again, to give her the answer to her dreams. "Why couldn't you ask me?"

"Because I'm a porcupine and you're Son of Light—strong and wise. A professional hero." She gave him a quick kiss. "And there's one more thing about last night."

"Which is?"

"I'd like to do it again. As soon as possible."

"That can be arranged."

He wished he could spend the rest of the day in her arms, watching her smile and listening to her lecture him about the geology of the area. And he wasn't done with the topic of their nonrelationship.

Unfortunately, he couldn't ignore the cold, hard threat of reality. "We should get going."

"Right." She stepped away from him. "There's no need to rush to the dig site for their coffee. It tastes like formaldehyde."

"There's instant coffee in the camper." Not very appealing but he needed the caffeine. "One of the other agents went to the grocery for us yesterday and picked up supplies. Stuff for sandwiches. A package of granola bars. I think there are doughnuts."

"Mmmmm." She rubbed her slender tummy. "Doughnuts."

While she returned to the camper, he strolled toward the rock ledge. Dash had attempted to use the elf-sized bathroom in the camper last night. He preferred the great outdoors. As he relieved himself, he gazed across the tops of pine trees and listened to the morning sounds of birds and chipmunks. Nothing dangerous here. Not like the road that lay ahead.

He needed to focus on Russell, but his thoughts returned to Cara. A porcupine? Not in his opinion. Last night, she hadn't been prickly.

Back in the camper, he sipped the barely palatable instant coffee and munched doughnuts. He shoved everything else from his mind. Time to change gears. Time to do his job. "I have a question for you, Cara."

"Shoot."

"When Russell held you captive, you said you heard another voice. Any chance you could identify the speaker?"

"Doubtful. I had the impression that it was another man, that's all."

"I have to consider the possibility that Russell isn't working alone. He might be using one of his buddies from the dig site."

"Hard to believe," she said. "Russell never was much of a leader. Even among the archaeology nerds, he was pegged as a loner."

"I've checked the criminal records on the other people at the site. Two of the young men have minor offenses." Not exactly gang-bangers. These college students were mostly clean. "Is there anything else you remember about that voice?"

Her brow furrowed as she tried to concentrate. He wished he could see inside her head, to really understand her needs. Damn it, he could make room in his life for her. If necessary, he'd hire movers to clear out all his old baggage.

"Angry," she said. "The voice was angry and demanding."

"In what way?"

"I can't be certain. I was hallucinating like crazy. But I had a sense that the other person was giving the orders. Russell sounded sad. And very young." Her lips pursed, and she set the doughnut down on a paper plate. "It sounds crazy to say this, but he had a very sweet side to his personality. When I had him in class, he reminded me of a puppy dog."

Dash hadn't abandoned his idea that the

other person—the man giving the orders—was William Graff, Russell's father. Before they went to the dig site, he needed to contact Flynn and have him check on the elder Graff's whereabouts.

Talking to Flynn wouldn't be easy. Dash hadn't exactly explained his plan to take Cara with him to the dig site, and he was damn sure that Flynn wouldn't approve of the risk. Unless he got results.

AS THEY DROVE NEARER to the dig site on the Colorado side of the Four Corners region, Cara recognized familiar landmarks. A barren hillside destroyed by a forest fire. A towering rock formation. Compared to the arid plains of the reservation, this landscape was almost verdant with an abundance of pine, scrub oak, aspen and shrubs.

Russell had promised to find her here.

Though she'd locked the memory of her abduction into a dark corner of her mind, a glimmer of fear shone through and she looked toward Dash for reassurance. In his strong profile, she saw little resemblance to the man who had tenderly made love to her in their camper mini-home. Last night, he'd been attentive to her every whim. He'd grinned and teased and nibbled her earlobe.

This morning, his attitude was determined and a little bit fierce. A professional hero. A man who would never settle down. Though she wished their relationship could be different, she accepted him for who he was. Son of Light, strong and wise; he would always come to her rescue.

"Do you think Russell will show himself?"

"I doubt it," he said. "Not in broad daylight."

"Then why are we coming here?"

"The people at the site have been interviewed by one of our other agents, but they might open up to you. They might give you a clue."

His jaw tightened. He hadn't shaved this morning and probably not the day before. His light stubble looked rough and sexy. And yet, underlying his tension, she sensed that he was enjoying himself. Tracking down bad guys was what he did for a living.

And she was a professor. Her lifework didn't require overt courage. She wiped her sweaty palms on her jeans. Though she wanted to be part of the investigation, she was having second thoughts. "Are we making a mistake by coming here?"

"Flynn seems to think so. When I told him about the note you found in your term papers, he was ready to mobilize the search teams and choppers to blanket this area."

"Not a bad idea."

"It's crap," he said. "The manhunt failed. Russell's too smart. He knows how to hide. The only way we'll catch him is face-to-face."

They were almost there. The camper rounded the edge of a mesa and descended into a wide box canyon. The cliff dwelling perched in a high rock crevice, facing east to catch the first rays of the sun. It hadn't been well preserved; only a few walls of the adobe brick structures remained. More interesting were the ruins of other houses and hogans scattered across this wide area that was sheltered on three sides by hills and cliffs. Research showed this had been a farming community. The cliff houses—well-stocked with provisions—provided a fortress in case of attack or siege by an enemy tribe.

The area where the archaeologists had set up camp included several motor homes. The largest held the sensitive instruments and chemicals used by Dr. Sterling in his forensic anthropology investigation. Another was used for cooking and utility. The two smaller motor homes provided sleeping quarters for Dr. Sterling and Dr. George Petty, who was in charge of the site. The students—their number varied from six to twelve—slept in twelve-foot-long canvas tents with wood floors.

Before they reached the parking area, Dash pulled onto the shoulder and stopped. His expression was serious. "We don't have to do this, Cara. If you're worried, we can turn around and go back to the safe house."

"A minute ago you told me that Russell probably won't show himself."

"Probably not. He's a stalker who picks out his prey and waits for the right moment to approach. He won't initiate a direct confrontation."

"Especially not with you."

Above all, Russell had shown himself to be prudent. He'd hidden from the searchers. Except for the deputy he'd shot in the leg, he saved his violence for women—unsuspecting women like her who were unable to defend themselves. His victims. *She couldn't let them down.* Cara thought of the burned remains at Mesa Verde—a charred skeleton that had once been a living woman. And the Navajo elder's daughter.

Russell would strike again unless she and Dash could stop him. She met his gaze. "I want to be here."

"You're a brave little porcupine." His breathtaking blue eyes shimmered. For a moment, his tough-guy facade slipped, and she saw the man who had passionately made love to her. "This is all going to turn out all right."

She wished she had half his confidence. "Tell me what I should do."

"Talk to his friends. Find out if any of them knew what he was doing. And listen to their voices. One of them might be the second person who was with Russell."

She shuddered at the thought. One of these students might have seen her tied up and helpless.

"Concentrate on his girlfriend," Dash advised. "Find out why she sent us that message."

"Catch you later?" Despite herself, she shivered.

"He'll never catch you, Cara. I won't let that happen. After we're done here, I'm taking you back to the safe house."

"And you?"

"I'll be doing my job." Dash needed to be more active in the manhunt. No more creeping around the edges and waiting for other people to act. He wanted Russell in custody, locked up where he couldn't hurt anyone else.

He started the camper and drove the rest of the way into the encampment. As soon as he parked, people were approaching the vehicle. There was a sameness in the way they were dressed in worn, baggy jeans, khakis and sweatshirts. Shaggy hair. Thick-soled hiking boots.

These were the archaeology nerds, and Cara was the best person to talk to them. Immediately, they circled around her, babbling excitedly. When she introduced them to Dash, they studied him with the guarded curiosity of people who had never met a real-life FBI agent before. Basically, they appeared to be decent kids. Dash reminded himself that appearances could be deceiving; Russell had been one of these kids. A puppy dog. Except when he was abducting and murdering young women.

As they gathered around a picnic table, Dr. George Petty approached. He was an older man, fit and ruddy-faced. A black knit cap was pulled low on his forehead. When he shook Dash's hand, his grip was strong. "How can I help you, Agent Adams?"

"Tell me about a typical day at the site. If Russell Graff were here, what would he be doing right now?"

"Poor Russell." George Petty frowned. "He seemed to be a nice young man. Perhaps a bit of a loner. But from a very good family. He's very fond of his mother."

"Why do you think that?"

"He talked about her often. And he carried a photograph of the two of them on a vacation."

"What about his father?"

"Never mentioned him. Such a nice young man." Petty shook his head. "That's what people always say, isn't it? When they found Son of Sam, the neighbors said he was a pleasant fellow. A mail carrier."

Which was exactly the way Dash would have described Dr. Petty. A pleasant fellow. Was it a pose? Was he the second voice Cara had heard?

Dash glanced back at the picnic table where she was deep in conversation with the students. She fit in well. In spite of what she'd said about not having a place where she belonged, everyone here seemed to accept her.

He'd noticed the same thing on the reservation. Everywhere she went, people welcomed her. They cared about her. Living alone had been a choice she'd made for herself. And now she wanted a family. A husband. Shouldn't be a problem. Other guys would line up around the block for the opportunity to give her a home—an image he found intensely irritating.

"Could I interest you in a cup of coffee?" Petty asked.

He remembered Cara's comment about formaldehyde. "No, thanks."

"Well, then. You wanted to hear about our work."

"Yes."

As Dr. Petty explained about excavations and artifacts, mapping and sectioning, Dash surveyed the surroundings, noticing many good hiding places among the rocks and trees. The high-topped mesa with the cliff dwelling was to the east. The western side of this U-shaped canyon was a forested hillside. He spotted an aspen grove, a sign of ground-water. "Excuse me, Dr. Petty. Is there a creek in this area?"

"Indeed, there is." He pointed toward the north wall of the canyon. "The creek comes through the rocks over there. This excellent water source was diverted into irrigation ditches by the ancient people. They were good farmers. At one time, there might have been upwards of five hundred people living here."

"Russell worked with Dr. Sterling."

"On the burial mounds and in the cliff dwelling where they've found evidence of a great battle."

"Has Dr. Sterling returned?"

"As far as I know, he's still in Window Rock."

He saw Cara rise from the picnic table and come toward them. After she warmly greeted George Petty, she turned to Dash. "May I speak with you for a moment?"

Her tone was so formal that he almost laughed out loud. Last night, she'd been screaming his name in the heat of their passionate lovemaking. He matched her attitude as he turned to Petty. "Please excuse us."

They were only a few steps away when she said, "Nobody has seen Joanne Jones this morning."

"Russell's girlfriend. Do you think they ran off together?"

"Or something might have happened to her." Cara set off in the direction of the canvas tents with quick strides. "What if he hurt her?"

Joanne was a redhead, not typical of Russell's usual victims. But his actions were increasingly hard to predict. He'd killed that blond woman. "How do you know which tent is Joanne's?"

"The women's tent is separate from the others. Right now, there's only Joanne and one other female. She wasn't sure whether Joanne even came to bed last night."

"Why didn't she inform Dr. Petty?"

"It's not unusual for Joanne to stay out all night. Apparently, she's a bit of a dig-site slut."

"Were you aware of this before?"

"Not really," Cara said. "Joanne certainly doesn't look the part. Thin and petite. When she wears her hair in braids, she could be twelve years old."

Inside the tent were four cots covered with sleeping bags. Suitcases and feminine gear were stowed underneath. Cara pointed to a redheaded Raggedy Ann doll on one of the beds. "That has to be Joanne's."

Dash expertly rifled through her belongings. Tucked between the sleeping bag and the mattress, he found a single sheet of white paper. The spacing was similar to the note Cara had received. The message was typed. Dash read it aloud. "Meet me tonight at the place of long shadows."

"Oh no." Her hand flew to cover her mouth. "She wouldn't be that foolish."

Dash cursed himself for being unprepared. He hadn't planned for another abduction. "Where is it? This place of long shadows?"

"To the north. Near the creek. I'll take you there."

Which was exactly what Russell wanted, to lure Cara closer. "Unacceptable. I'll go alone."

"It's not easy to locate."

And what would he do with her while he was searching? He couldn't leave her alone and unguarded. Even if she was locked inside the camper, Russell had a gun and could shoot out the windows. Nor could he entrust her safety to the other students. For all he knew, these kids had banded together to hide Russell.

He pulled his cell phone from his jacket pocket. "I'm calling for backup."

Russell had obviously set up an ambush, and Dash cursed himself for falling into this trap. He contacted Flynn, informed him of the situation and requested helicopter backup and other searchers.

"We're in luck," he told Cara. "There's a chopper at the safe house. They should be here in a half hour to forty minutes."

"Not fast enough," she said. "And what if he's holding her captive? What if the sound of the helicopter makes him angry and causes him to…do something terrible."

Dash had never met Joanne Jones. If the Raggedy Ann doll on the bed was any clue to her personality, she was probably a childish, perhaps clueless young woman. But she didn't deserve to die for that.

"Half an hour to forty minutes," he repeated.

"He's close, Dash. I can feel it." Her tone was urgent. "If something happens to Joanne because of me, I'll never forgive myself."

Her words stirred his blood. He could end Russell's deadly games right now. His instincts told him that he might never have another chance as good as this. Russell was out there, waiting. He could be caught. "Let's go."

They left the tent without a word to anyone else and jogged toward the north end of the canyon, toward the creek. Dash moved at a quick pace. His senses were on high alert as he scanned the territory, watching for any sign of Russell.

The creek rushed and shimmered in the morning sunlight. It was only a few feet wide, a narrow swath that cut through high shrubs and buffalo grass. He noticed a footprint at the edge. Not much of a clue with all these people on site.

"It's uphill from here," Cara said.

He glanced back over his shoulder and saw no one. Nothing. He drew the Glock from his shoulder holster.

This pursuit was unlike most of his prior experience. For the most part, Dash had been based in cities where searches took place amid streetlights and concrete buildings. Out here in nature there were many more places to hide. The irregular shapes of rocks and trees easily disguised the human form.

Russell could be watching them right now. He could be as close as the leafy stand of aspen to their left. Or laying atop a distant mesa, watching them through binoculars.

Wind rustled through the trees. Light and shadow shifted. The pattern of the landscape changed. To locate Russell, Dash needed to rely on more than his vision. Sense of smell? Sound?

As he moved forward, he listened to the twittering of small animals and birds. The wind. The rushing of the creek. A twig snapped. To his left? He shot a gaze in that direction and saw nothing but a thick shrub.

He needed to use his brain. His logic. Assuming that Russell's plan was to capture Cara, he must have also planned an escape route. But there were no roads leading into this area. Where would he park his car?

Dash closed the distance between himself and Cara until he was right on her heels.

"We're here," she said.

Directly in front of them was a boulder the size of a Hummer. Crude carvings showed stick figures holding spears and dancing. Long shadows stretched out behind them.

Other massive boulders leaned against the pictograph rock and the creek spilled out between them. Dash was looking into the maw of a cave.

More than likely, Russell was in there. He'd already chosen his position, hidden in the dark. He was armed. Walking into his lair would be a suicide mission.

Cara whispered, "Do we go in there?"

"Hell, no."

If he'd been alone, Dash would have taken the risk. He was an ace marksman, and he'd match his hand-to-hand combat skills against Russell any day. But Cara was with him. He wouldn't take a chance with her life.

Looking down, he noticed something half-buried in the dirt at the foot of the pictographs. Quickly, he stepped forward and brushed the dirt away. A hunting knife with a leather handle.

Cara crouched beside him, staring down at the blade. "It looks like the same knife he left in the room with me. When I was his captive."

Russell had left it behind. Another reminder. Another threat.

Chapter Fifteen

When the other agents arrived, Cara insisted on riding in the helicopter with Dash. Though her heart pounded wildly and her common sense told her to back off, she needed to be part of this action, to find Joanne Jones. The poor girl must be terrified. Or worse. Would he kill her? Would they find her remains in a fire pit?

Fear gnawed inside Cara. Not for herself, but for Joanne.

Dash sat beside her in the search-and-rescue chopper. She listened through earphones while he gave instructions to the pilot and the other agent onboard. After his brief description of Joanne Jones, he turned to her. "Anything else, Cara?"

"She might be purposely trying to hide. Russell was her boyfriend."

"No accounting for taste," Dash muttered.

Thinking of her own experience with Russell, Cara added, "And she might be drugged."

As they lifted off, she looked down at the students and George Petty. Dash considered them to be suspicious persons, but she didn't believe that characterization. Not only had they been friendly to her, but they were scientists. In their minds, Russell's behavior was an anomaly—a deviation from the norm. He wasn't someone they identified with or wanted to emulate.

She pressed her fingertips against the chopper's window. The surface was cold, but she hardly registered that sensation. With all her might, she concentrated on searching for a glimpse of red hair, a flash of color. As they skimmed above treetops, the ground below seemed to pass too quickly for her to focus. They looped in a wide circle toward the high mesa above the cliff dwellings—a view that should have given her solace and peace.

She tried to remember her former academic innocence, when danger was a distant thought that didn't apply to her everyday life. Centuries ago, the *dineh* had sought refuge from their enemies inside those cliff dwellings. What would those ancient people have thought if they'd seen a helicopter? Some of the Hopi pictographs showed people in flying machines, actually, and...

"Head around to the west," Dash instructed. "Nice and slow."

She knew that he was taking them to the rock with the long shadow figures. Russell's designated meeting place. When they'd stood outside that rock cave, she'd known he was there. Waiting for her with his soft cotton rope and his stun gun. Remembered pain rose from the scar on her arm. Poor Joanne.

Even more than with the other victims, Cara felt direct responsibility for this abduction. Russell had callously played on Joanne's affection for him, using her to send them a message.

Dash pointed through the chopper window. "There she is."

Cara looked down. On the top of the boulders where the pictographs were carved, she saw red-haired Joanne Jones. Her wrists and ankles were bound. She was moving. Struggling to her knees, she raised her hands toward the chopper in a plea for help.

"I can't land here," the pilot said. "There's not enough space on that rock and too many trees."

Below, Joanne flopped down. She was perilously close to the edge of the rock. "She might be hallucinating," Cara said. "We can't leave her alone here."

"Sorry, ma'am," the pilot said. "I can drop down pretty low, but there's no place for a safe landing. I think I saw a clearing back toward the east."

"I'll get her," Dash said. "Got a rope ladder?"

"Sure do, but I don't advise making the descent. Not with an armed fugitive in the area."

"I concur," said the other agent. "He could be waiting down there in the trees to pick you off."

"So I'll wear a Kevlar vest."

Dash dug through equipment and hauled out a white rope ladder with plastic rungs that looked like gear from a children's playground. Certainly not substantial enough for dangling from a helicopter. Cara didn't like this plan. Not at all.

But when she looked down, she saw Joanne raising her tied wrists, trying to stand up. The wind from the hovering blades churned the tops of pine trees at the edge of the high rocks. If Russell had drugged Joanne with the same hallucinogen he'd used with Cara, the girl must be terrified.

An echo of that fear resonated in Cara's chest as she watched Dash. She hated that he was exposing himself to possible gunfire. Danger was the downside to being a hero.

When he opened the hatch and prepared to descend, she wanted to cling to him. At least to give him a kiss for luck. As he fastened the vest over his shirt, his gaze met hers. She mouthed the words, "Be careful."

In response he gave her a reckless grin. *Damn his job. And damn him for enjoying it.*

He climbed down the ladder.

The other agent positioned himself and aimed his rifle into the trees. Cara couldn't imagine how he'd get a decent shot with the constant vibration.

Holding her breath, she watched as Dash stepped from rung to rung. Dangling in midair with no way to defend himself, he made an easy target.

She peered into the surrounding craggy rocks, searching for the glint of sun against a gun barrel. Fear tensed her body. *Don't let anything happen to him. Please, keep him safe.*

She prayed to Father Sun and the winds of the north, to all who had gone before. Anyone who would listen.

He dropped onto the rock surface and crouched. So far, so good.

Immediately, he went to Joanne. Using a pocketknife, he cut through her bonds. As soon as she was free, she wrapped her thin arms around him, but Dash paid little attention. He was staring at a crevice in the rocks.

"He sees something," the pilot said.

The agent with the rifle angled around. "I can't tell what it is."

What was he looking at? Cara couldn't see. The angle was wrong. Pure dread clenched her heart. She couldn't bear to lose him. They had only begun to know each other, to care for each other.

Dash positioned Joanne in a harness. When she was secure, he ducked low, ran toward the crevice and returned carrying a backpack. Holding on to the ladder, he signaled for them to pull him up.

In minutes, he and Joanne spilled into the chopper. They were safe.

For now, he was safe.

WHEN THE CHOPPER TOUCHED DOWN at the dig site to drop off Cara and Dash, Joanne climbed out, too. She clung desperately to Cara's arm. Her complexion was pale. Her eyes frightened. "You've got to help me, Dr. Messinger. I want to go home."

"I understand." Cara had felt the same way after she'd escaped from Russell. All she had wanted was to be left alone to lick her wounds in private. "It's really for the best, Joanne. These agents will take you to a hospital."

Cara saw the other students from the dig site rushing toward them. This hadn't been part of the plan. The chopper was supposed to stop here only long enough to drop off Cara and Dash, then take Joanne to the hospital in Durango where she could be questioned.

Dash came toward them. "Joanne, you need to get back in the helicopter."

"I'm afraid." She tightened her grip on Cara's arm. "I want Dr. Messinger with me. I need her."

"Maybe you two should talk." He made eye contact with Cara. "Joanne might want to tell you things that she couldn't say to anyone else."

Clearly, he wanted her to question Joanne,

to dig for information. She gave him a quick nod as she patted Joanne's shoulder. "You can talk to me."

"Thank you, Dr. Messinger."

While Dash held everyone else back, she guided Joanne along the road leading away from the dig site. They walked slowly—one halting step at a time. The whir of the helicopter blades faded behind them. Gently, Cara said, "I know you've had a rough time. Talking about it helps."

"Okay."

"Tell me what happened."

Though the redhead was only a few inches shorter than Cara, her frail frame made her seem childlike. Her voice was little more than a whisper. "I got a note from Russell to meet him at the long shadows rock. And I went there last night after everybody else was asleep."

Even though she knew Russell was dangerous. Now wasn't the time for Cara to scold. "Go on."

Her thin lips pinched. "People were saying terrible things about him. But I didn't believe them. He was my boyfriend."

"How did he get to the site? We didn't see his car."

"He has a motorcycle. A dirt bike."

"What happened when you met him?"

"He wouldn't talk. And he wouldn't touch me, either. We just sat there in that stupid cave."

Cara thought of her own experience with Russell. The drugs. "Did he give you anything to eat or drink?"

"No, he ignored me. We must have been there an hour. And then I told him that I was cold and tired and he was a jerk. And then… He was so…" She stopped walking. "He told me I wasn't worth the bother. I was nothing. Nobody."

Sobbing, she flung herself into Cara's arms. She was so thin. Her bones were as delicate as a bird's. Silently, Cara cursed Russell for hurting this vulnerable girl. "You're going to be all right."

"I was so stupid." Joanne swiped at her tears. "Why did I trust him?"

"Everybody makes mistakes." And this was a doozy. At least Joanne was still alive. She'd have a chance to put her life back together.

"When he tied me up," she said, "I knew the things they were saying about him were true. He was like a different person, and he scared me."

"When did he take you up on top of the rock?"

"This morning. He untied my ankles so I could walk and when we got up there, he tied my legs again."

Cara remembered the knots that had bound her wrists. Climbing over rocks would have been nearly impossible with those restraints. "He didn't untie your hands?"

"I don't think so."

The girl's memory lapse seemed unlikely. Was Joanne lying to her? "Did you try to climb down?"

"Russell told me not to move. If I did, he said he'd punish me."

"You didn't try?"

"Was that wrong?"

Her watery eyes searched Cara's face. Looking for absolution? Or for something else?

There was one more issue Cara needed to discuss. "You sent me a message, Joanne. Yesterday, you told Dr. Sterling that you needed to see me and you would 'catch me later.' What did that mean?"

Her gaze flicked left and right, looking for a way to avoid giving an answer. "I don't know."

"Of course, you do." Cara wouldn't let her hide from the truth. "Russell told you to say that."

"I guess so."

"When did you see him?"

"He called me." She stuck her hand into her pant's pocket and took out a cell phone. "I have to ask you a favor, Dr. Messinger. A big one."

"I'm listening."

"Russell told me there was one more thing I had to do for him." She pushed the cell phone into Cara's hand. "I'm supposed to give this to you. You have to keep it with you all the time, and you can't tell anyone you have it."

So this was the plan. Russell had never intended to kill his red-haired girlfriend; he needed her alive to hand over the cell phone. Had this been his goal all along? Had he drawn them into this chase for no other reason than to open a line of communication with Cara?

"You can't tell anybody," Joanne said. "If you do, Russell will come back and hurt me. Please, Dr. Messinger. You've got to promise."

Time for Joanne to grow up. To put away the Raggedy Ann dolls and develop a sense of responsibility. "I won't make that promise."

"You have to." She actually looked surprised. "Russell wanted me to—"

"You're still helping him." This skinny little girl was trying to con her. "Listen to me, Joanne. Russell doesn't deserve your help. And certainly not your trust."

"But he loves me."

Cara could hardly believe her ears. "He hurt you. Abused you. That's not love."

Her words set off another storm of tears. Though Cara felt sympathy, she wouldn't allow herself to be drawn into another of Russell's complicated schemes. This phone would go directly from her hand to Dash's.

AFTER JOANNE HAD BEEN SAFELY tucked into the helicopter on her way to a hospital and protective custody, Dash advised Dr. Petty and his crew to take precautions. Any contact from Russell needed to be reported immediately.

Back in the camper with Cara, he drove toward the safe house where he'd be required to file a report on this incident. Another botched attempt. He should have figured that Russell would return to the dig. He should have ordered heavy surveillance to be posted all over that site from the very first day of the search.

Damn it. He hated to lose. His mood was dark, filled with self-recrimination. And the weather reflected his frustration. Storm clouds had rolled in, blanketing the skies. The air was heavy with moisture.

"Why the hell does he make everything so complicated?" Once again, Russell had led them on a Byzantine and ultimately useless chase. "That whole weird thing with switching the cars. Now, this fake abduction."

"He never planned to hurt Joanne," Cara said. "The whole point was to give me the cell phone."

"There are easier ways."

"Not in his mind," she said. "Remember what Dr. Treadwell said? This is a control thing. He wants to make you jump through hoops."

"He's doing a damn good job of it." If Dash had been keeping score, all the points would have been chalked up on Russell's side of the board. "I hate the way he's playing us."

"That's not what worries me," she said. "If Joanne wasn't really abducted, it doesn't count."

"For what?"

"Russell promised to punish one person a day. He might take another victim."

Though Dash hoped one encounter was enough for the day, she was right. They should expect the worst.

He checked the rearview mirror. The last thing he needed right now was for Russell to follow them to the safe house. If a serial killer discovered the location, safe-house security would be compromised.

There were no other vehicles on the road behind them. No cars. No motorcycles.

The first raindrop hit the windshield with a splat. If the rain picked up, helicopter search in the area would be curtailed. Nothing was going right.

He glanced toward Cara. "You did a good job talking to Joanne."

"She makes me sad." She shrugged as if she could shake off that feeling.

"Knowing that Russell has a dirt bike is helpful." He could go to places where there were no roads, but the bike would leave tire tracks. "I put out an APB."

"You never told me what was in that backpack you picked up on the rock."

"Russell's laptop."

"Oh, my." She gasped with surprise. "Why on earth would he leave that behind?"

"He meant for us to find it so I suspect it's the start to another wild-goose chase. But he might have outsmarted himself this time. Our forensic computer experts can mine a lot of data from that machine."

"Like what?"

"The times he logged on. Locations. Routing patterns. Sites he's visited. This data creates mathematical probabilities about what he's planning to do next."

"More experts?" She scoffed. "Why bother?"

He didn't blame her for being cynical. Nothing had worked against Russell. Not crime-scene forensics. Not psychological profiling. "I'll admit that our high-level technical advice hasn't been real successful."

"A complete failure."

"Is there any grade lower than an F?"

"I'm not blaming you, Dash. Nor anyone else. I'm usually the first person in line to trust the opinion of experts, but nothing seems to be working. Nothing makes sense. Like Joanne." She huffed an angry sigh. "I can't believe she still has feelings for Russell."

"Joanne wouldn't be the first woman to fall in love with a monster."

"But it's so irrational."

Her logic brought a smile to his lips. Only Cara—the total academic—would demand rationality from emotion. "I don't think love is supposed to make sense."

"Of course, it does. Initial physical attractions can be quantified and measured. Establishing a relationship takes a great deal of measured planning."

"How do you quantify a kiss?"

She fidgeted in the passenger seat. "Accelerated pulse rate. Increased sensory stimulation. It can all be analyzed."

Last night when they'd made love, she hadn't been analyzing. "People in love are supposed to be overwhelmed, swept off their feet."

"In fairy tales."

When he glanced toward her, he felt the pull of that magic called love. With every moment he spent with her, she seemed more ideal. "I thought you were the one who believed in fairy tales—all those myths and legends."

"I've studied them," she admitted.

"So you know that love doesn't always

make sense. Cupid draws back his bow and zaps unlikely lovers. Like an archaeology professor and an FBI agent."

A faint blush colored her cheeks, and her full lips smiled as she said, "What could possibly be more irrational?"

"Ignoring the attraction."

He wouldn't make that mistake.

RUSSELL SAT IN THE SHADOW of an overhanging rock ledge watching as the rain splattered on the dark red earth. He hugged his knees, making himself into a ball. Slowly, he rocked back and forth. He was lonely and wanted Cara to be with him, cradling his head against her breast and singing to him.

If Joanne had done as he'd told her, he'd talk to Cara today. But there were long hours stretching in front of him and so many other things he had to do. "I miss my computer."

You had to get rid of it. The time was right.

"I'm bored." When he was a boy, his mother had always told him to find something to occupy his mind. To quit bothering her. She was very busy. On the phone. Getting dressed up in lace and satin. "I'm bored."

Find yourself a hobby, little boy. Make yourself useful.

"I collect things."

Insects and rodents. A cat. A robin. It had started when his class had gone to the museum and had seen insects pinned to a board so they could be studied. He'd done the same, piercing their hard little shells with a long pin from his mother's diamond brooch.

He'd watched them die. Their souls belonged to him. Just as Cara would be his.

She wants to be with you. To die in your arms.

He pushed the hair off his forehead and looked out at the gray, drizzling rain.

Chapter Sixteen

By the time Dash parked the camper in front of the safe house, the rain was falling steadily. Glumly, he stared through the windshield. "I'll see if I can find an umbrella in here somewhere."

"No problem." Cara pushed open her door.

"You're going to get wet."

"Then I'll dry off again." She flashed him a dazzling smile. "I like the rain."

She ran toward the house with her black hair flipping gracefully behind her. Ironically, she seemed to draw strength from each new disaster.

Grabbing a few things from the camper, he followed her to the covered front porch where Grace Lennox sat in a rocking chair. She was reading a book with Yazzie draped across her lap.

Cara reached down to stroke the scruffy orange fur. "How was he, Grace? Did he miss me?"

Before she could answer, Yazzie spoke for himself. He let out a long, plaintive yowl. He rolled off Grace's lap and landed on the porch with a clunk. Then he bashed against Cara's shins. She scooped Yazzie up and held him so she was looking directly into his eyes. "Good grief," she said. "He feels even heavier than before."

"Nothing wrong with his appetite," Grace said. "How was your tribal council meeting?"

"Oh my God. So much has happened that I almost forgot. It went very well. Everyone agreed that there was a need for more police presence at the casinos, and more social programs to deal with the gamblers."

Dash asked, "How were things around here?"

"Flynn has been in a perfectly dreadful mood." She carefully placed a bookmark in the pages and closed her book. "I think he's upset with you, Agent Adams."

"No doubt," he said.

"On the plus side, that charming psychologist, Jonas Treadwell, is here, and he'll certainly be staying for lunch."

With all that had happened this morning, Dash could hardly believe it was only noon. Six hours ago, he'd been standing on a cliff with Cara, hearing her tell him that he deserved an A-plus for his sexual performance. Since then, everything had crashed and burned.

Dash wasn't looking forward to this confrontation with Flynn, but he couldn't put it off. "Excuse me, ladies."

Flynn was waiting in the front room. He sat in one of the heavy armchairs near the fireplace. His eyes narrowed in a squint as he nodded a greeting.

Dash sat opposite him. "From what I hear, you're in a perfectly dreadful mood."

"How about you?"

"Been better," Dash said. "I blew it." He held his arms wide, inviting Flynn to take his best shot. He deserved the reprimand. He'd gone into a dangerous situation alone, putting Cara in danger. "All the waiting around and getting nowhere was making me crazy. I needed to go after him."

"You followed a hunch. Took a risk."

"I played right into his hands."

Flynn rose slowly. He seemed exhausted, sleep-deprived. Resting an elbow on the mantel, he looked down at Dash. "Now you know how it feels. I was after the Judge for a year. A whole year when he killed seven women. No matter what I did, he was always one step ahead." He stopped abruptly and shrugged. "You know the story."

He sure as hell did. The pressure and the guilt had destroyed Flynn. Dash refused to let the same thing happen to him. Through the screen door leading to the porch, he heard Cara's laughter as she chatted. More than anything, he wanted to keep her safe. "We need to start processing the information we got from the site."

Flynn nodded. "We'll debrief with Treadwell in the den. Bring Cara, too."

Dash stepped back onto the porch. Slate-gray skies and sheets of rain formed a dull backdrop. In contrast, Cara seemed to shine. Her eyes were gray pearls. Her white teeth flashed. "Come with me. We need to talk with Treadwell."

"Lucky you," Grace said. She fluttered her hand as if she were fanning her face. "Find out if he likes older women."

Cara patted her arm. "I'll put in a good word for you."

Yazzie preceded them into the house. He

swaggered toward the kitchen. The cat had the right idea; Dash would have killed for a decent cup of coffee, but there were more pressing concerns.

As he walked beside Cara toward the den, he slipped his arm around her slim waist. He wanted to tell her how important she was to him, how he wanted to be with her forever. All kinds of *irrational* thoughts crashed around inside his brain. He wanted to say that he could be the man she needed, that they belonged together. But those weren't the words that came out of his mouth. "I might not have mentioned this lately, but you are very hot."

She tossed her head. "Is that an expert opinion?"

"I've had some experience."

"So have I." She patted his butt.

In the den, Dash and Cara greeted Treadwell. In his red knit shirt and khakis, he might have just stepped off a golf course. Immediately, Cara started pitching the charms of Grace Lennox.

Dash interrupted. "We need to get started. First, there's this." He held up the cell phone. "Russell went to a lot of trouble to open this line of communication to Cara. We need to be ready for his call."

Flynn went to the door and called to Wesley, the resident electronics expert.

"And this." Dash held up the backpack he'd retrieved when he'd rescued Joanne. "Russell left us his laptop computer."

"I don't get it," Flynn said. "Why?"

"Leaving clues seems to be his new thing." Dash reached into the pack and pulled out the plastic-wrapped hunting knife. "Cara identified this knife. It's the one he had when he was holding her captive."

Treadwell came closer to get a better look. "He's left other items behind."

"A ceremonial pipe," Dash said. That had been at Mesa Verde near the body. "And eagle feathers. And there was a bowl with his thumbprint at the lodge where his father was staying in Durango."

"He's divesting himself of precious objects," Treadwell said. "This isn't good."

"What does it mean?"

"It signals a change." He lowered himself onto the leather sofa. "The Judge is invested in his rituals. His satisfaction comes from doing the same thing, over and over. He always looks for the same physical characteristics in his victims. He stalks them, then holds them for four days."

"Like he did with me," Cara said.

"When you escaped, you interrupted his script."

"But he killed again," Dash said. "The woman at Mesa Verde."

"That murder was different. He didn't hold her for the ritual four days. And there are other behavioral anomalies. He used a gun when he shot the deputy," Treadwell pointed out. "He captured one woman and didn't kill her. The blonde didn't fit his profile victim. Several distinctly different behaviors."

Dash was well aware that the serial killer pattern had changed. "The only constant is his obsession with Cara."

"True."

"Can you tell me what Russell is going to do next?"

"If I had a crystal ball."

Treadwell gave him a genial smile as if friendliness could defuse the tension that had taken root in Dash's gut. He was glad when Wesley came into the room. Though this newbie agent was dressed like a cowboy, his language was high-tech.

If he hooked the cell phone into a global scan and trace, they might be able to triangulate on Russell's position. "But that's going to take some time," Wesley said. "Right now, we can use the speaker function if Russell calls. Cara needs to stay close. He'll expect to hear her voice."

He took the laptop to the table by the window and booted up. They might as well take a look before they passed this on to the computer geniuses who could track all the data.

Finally, Dash sensed that they were making forward progress. He turned back to Treadwell. "All these changes Russell is making, do they point toward anything?"

"Suicide."

Hard to believe. "I'm not a profiler, but I haven't seen any sign of remorse from Russell."

"Suicide doesn't necessarily mean he's sorry for what he's done," Treadwell explained. "Russell is clearly fascinated by death. After he kills, he spends a great deal of time with his victim. Postmortem."

"And there was that note on the mirror," Cara said. "In the motel room with all those photos of me, it said, 'Mine in life. Mine in death.'"

"Suicide might be the final step in his

ritual," Treadwell said. "He's giving away all his important objects before he takes his own life."

Dash still didn't believe it. "Any other interpretations?"

"He might be planning to move. To start over."

A hell of a thought. Russell had access to money. He'd pulled almost forty thousand dollars from an account his father had known nothing about, and there was likely more where that had come from. "He could go anywhere."

"But not right away," Treadwell said. "He has unfinished business here. His threat to punish one person a day. And his obsession with Cara."

She seemed to take this statement calmly. If Dash hadn't known her so intimately, he might not have noticed the tightness in her shoulders. "Is Cara the only reason he's staying here?"

"One of the reasons," Treadwell said. "You are also part of Russell's obsession, Dash. So is Flynn."

"The mind games."

"It gives him a sense of power that was probably lacking in his upbringing. He acts out his rage at his mother by dominating and murdering women. Law-enforcement authorities represent his father, who was probably abusive."

"Let's talk about William Graff." Dash told them about his meeting with the elder Graff in Window Rock and his suspicion that Russell and his father might be working together. "You both remember that Cara said she heard a second voice while she was being held captive. An angry male voice."

"I've given this matter some thought," Treadwell said. "When Cara mentioned the other voice, I first assumed she was hallucinating, which is still a possibility. But there might be another person involved. A dominating personality."

"Like his father."

"The idea of father-son serial killers is fascinating. Unprecedented in my experience." Treadwell looked pleased. "But there could be someone else. Perhaps a mentor."

"Like Dr. George Petty at the dig site," Dash said. "Or Dr. Sterling."

"That's ridiculous," Cara said.

"Hey, I met Sterling. He's a dominating personality."

"But he didn't know Russell in San Francisco," she pointed out.

"Excuse me," Wesley said. "Flynn, you should take a look at this."

Dash followed Flynn to the computer where they stood behind Wesley's shoulder. Several files were listed. One was labeled with Flynn's name.

"Open it," he said tersely.

A map took shape on the screen. The area displayed was Cortez and it included the safe house. A note at the bottom said: "She's buried by the four aspens below La Rana."

"La Rana is a rock formation," Wesley said. "It's about six miles from here."

The carefully pinpointed location changed everything. Russell knew about the safe house. Security was compromised. With one computer message from an Internet café, Russell could send his map all across the country, exposing the safe house and destroying this entire operation.

Before Dash's eyes, Flynn aged ten years in a minute. This had to be his worst nightmare. The Judge had found him. He'd laid another victim at Flynn's doorstep.

WITHIN A FEW SHORT HOURS, the whole atmosphere of the safe house underwent a dramatic transformation. Cara stood at the window in the den, watching the mobilization of FBI forces. The decision had been made that the safe house was no longer to be treated as a secret location. This quiet little farmhouse had become the center of operations. The rain had stopped as suddenly as it had started. The sun beat down.

Though Dash had been telling her all along that there was a manhunt underway, she had no idea how much was entailed. Field agents carrying guns. Behavioral analysts. A forensic team who had deployed to La Rana where—as Russell had promised—another burned corpse had been found.

Though most of the operation was sequestered in the bunkhouse offices, Cara was in the den with an electronics specialist who was rigging the cell phone. Yazzie stood at her side, hissing furiously at these strangers who'd invaded his territory and occasionally lashing out at passing ankles.

Cara felt much the same way. Though she was gratified to see the efforts being made, all this organized confusion was rather unnerving. She eyed the phones spread across the desk in the den and wished she could call her mother. Just to hear a familiar voice.

It had been years since she'd felt the need to go back home. Her academic life separated her from the family she'd grown up with. Lately, she'd been resenting her half sister's wedding and the horrid peach-colored bridesmaid dress she'd be expected to wear. Right now, going home sounded wonderful and safe. And when her mother asked if there were any new men in her life, she might mention Dashiell Quincy Adams with his gorgeous blue eyes and his Plymouth Rock pedigree. Or maybe not.

When this was over, she doubted she would see Dash again. He'd return to San Francisco and his essentially dangerous job. In spite of their closeness and the most incredible sex she'd ever experienced, their relationship was over before it even got started.

He strode into the den. All business. The sexy stubble was gone. He'd traded his black leather jacket for a crisp white shirt that looked as if it had been ironed only moments ago and a necktie—the uniform of Super Fed.

"Thought you might want an update," he said.

"A briefing?" She really didn't enjoy his professional persona. "By all means."

"Dr. Sterling is here," he said. "As soon as we determined there were bones buried by the four aspens below La Rana, I suggested we contact him."

"Before the body was removed?"

"Yes, ma'am." His grin betrayed a hint of intimacy. Just a hint. "I've been paying attention to your archaeology lectures about burial sites and plant growth and indigenous insects. I knew Sterling could tell us more if we waited for him."

"Has he drawn any conclusions?"

"You know how he works. He won't give conclusions until he's ready. But he suggests that this victim was buried almost two years ago, shortly after Flynn took over at the safe house."

"That can't be a coincidence."

"The Judge knew Flynn was here. He left the remains close on purpose. Why he kept that murder a secret until now, I don't know."

She thought of Treadwell's analysis. Russell was giving up all his secrets. Preparing to move on. Or to kill himself. "How's Flynn doing?"

"He's holding together. Of course, he blames himself, but—"

"So do I. I feel guilty because he's hurting

people in my name. So do you." They were all willing to take responsibility for the deeds of a madman because he wouldn't. He killed with impunity. With malice. With pure evil. "I want this to be over."

"We all do."

At her feet, Yazzie growled.

They were all on edge. Glancing over her shoulder at the electronics expert who was busily adjusting various dials and monitors, she lowered her voice. "I'm not too impressed with all these agents running around, taking notes and coming up with theories. You and I—just the two of us—got closer to Russell than any of them."

"At the cave," he said.

"We should have gone after him." She frowned. "If I hadn't been there, you would have chased him down. You turned back because you were protecting me."

"You're right. I might have tried something as stupid as charging into an ambush where my opponent had all the advantage."

When he put it that way, she felt far less guilty for holding him back. "Being with me protected you."

"Which brings me to the next thing I need to talk about." Though he didn't touch her, she could feel him reaching out. "Treadwell has talked to the behavioral analyst team."

"The profiler and the other psychologist." Those two men had spent a rather intense fifteen minutes questioning her. Though their manner was intelligent, she found it hard to take them seriously. One was tall and heavy, and the other was skinny with high eyebrows. They reminded her of Laurel and Hardy.

"They talked about you," Dash said. "When Russell calls, he'll probably ask you to do something. To perform some kind of task."

She could see where this was leading. "And?"

"They think you can handle it. If you're willing, they want you involved."

To be used as bait. Ever since she'd escaped from Russell's clutches, Cara had known it would come to this. A final showdown with the monster. "Of course, I'll do it."

Chapter Seventeen

Cara couldn't tell whether Dash was pleased with her response. He should have expected her to agree. For the past several days, she'd told him over and over that she wanted to be part of the investigation. If it meant catching Russell, she wanted him to use her.

He signaled the electronics expert and said, "We'll be back in a minute."

Taking her hand, he pulled her down the hall. On the way, they passed Laurel and Hardy, but Dash didn't pause. He took her into the bathroom—the last private sanctuary in the safe house.

As soon as he closed the door, he pulled her close. His kiss was ferocious and hard. He pressed her up against the tiled wall opposite the sink until her breasts crushed against him. She felt the hard edge of his shoulder holster, reminding her of the danger that surrounded them.

This burst of passion was unexpected but so very welcome. She'd been longing for his touch, needing this release from the rising tension. Her tongue plunged into his mouth. Sudden heat exploded. She latched her leg with his, pulling him closer.

He ended the kiss. His breath was hot on her ear. "I want a future with you, Cara."

"A what?"

He looked into her eyes. "I want to spend time with you. Lots of time. I want to know you better."

"A relationship." Her heart was pounding so loudly that she couldn't think. "Why are you saying this now?"

"Because I want you."

Another kiss. His taste was becoming more familiar. And his scent—a mix of tweed and leather. As she succumbed to his demanding strength, she felt as if she'd always known him, as if she'd been waiting for him all her life.

"What do you say, Cara? Do we have a future?"

She struggled to think. Of course, a relationship was totally impossible. The logistics were all wrong. They both had careers that required long hours and travel. Not to mention the inherent danger of his job. Would she accept less? "I don't think so."

He separated from her and turned away. He braced his hands on the bathroom sink and looked into the mirror. In his reflection, she saw his confusion.

"What's the problem?" he asked. "All I'm saying is that I want to get to know you better. It's not like I'm proposing marriage."

But that was exactly what she wanted. A future that included a home and family. And a husband. Dash couldn't give that to her. "A casual relationship isn't what I want."

"It could be more. Sometimes, you have to take a risk."

"Don't you dare talk to me about risk." She yanked on his arm, turning him around to face her. "You're the one with the dangerous job."

As he stared at her, she saw the hurt in his eyes. It was killing her to reject him, but she didn't have enough time to be subtle. She continued, "You talk about a future together and wanting to get to know me when you're risking your life every day. What kind of relationship could we have?"

"My life isn't any more dangerous than a cop or a fireman. Or a corporate lawyer with a bleeding ulcer headed for a coronary."

"You're wearing a shoulder holster," she pointed out.

"And I'm a hell of a good marksman, which makes me safer than a lot of people."

Her heart told her that he was the one—the man she'd been waiting for all her life. He was strong and brave. Intelligent and sensitive.

He was also inherently unable and unwilling to settle down. She could never demand that he give up his career. A relationship with him under those conditions would only lead to disappointment. "I'm sorry, Dash. There are just too many obstacles."

"Not obstacles. Challenges." He caught hold of her arms, forcing her to confront him. "You can't give up on me, Cara. You're not a quitter."

Of all the ways he could have described her, that was the most accurate. She never gave up. Not in her academic career, not in her private life. But this wasn't about her. It was about him. "People don't change. You're not the marrying kind."

"The hell I'm not." Right there in the

bathroom, he dropped to one knee. "Marry me."

Looking down into the stunning blue of his eyes, she saw a man she could live with for the rest of her life. If she dared… If she was willing to take the chance…

There was a hammering on the bathroom door and a shout. "We need Cara. He's calling."

She flung open the door and rushed into the den. The behavioral analyst guys were standing by. The electronics expert pointed to her. "The line is open now. Talk."

Gasping, she said, "Hello?"

"Hi, Cara. It's me, Russell."

His voice sounded through the room. Everyone else was silent. "Hello, Russell."

"Have you missed me?" he asked. "I've missed you, but that's about to change. We're finally going to get together."

She looked toward Laurel and Hardy. They had instructed her on what to say. "I'm not free to come and go as I please. It might be better if you came to me."

"That sounds like something a psychologist would tell you to say." He laughed as though he didn't have a care in the world. "I hope you're not talking to some dumb shrink."

"Of course not."

"Because if you tell anybody about this… Well, that would suck. Big time."

He sounded so young. How could this be the same man who had brutally murdered those women? Who had kidnapped her? "I won't tell anyone."

"If you did, I might have to hurt this nice girl who's here with me. Do you want to talk to her?"

"Yes."

From the corner of her eye, she saw Dash. His jaw clenched. If he could have reached through the phone and strangled Russell, she had no doubt that he would have done so.

Then she heard the sobs of his next victim. The sound tore into her. "If you hurt her, Russell, you'll never see me again."

"No problem. I just wanted to show you I was serious."

"What do you want?"

"At six o'clock, you'll go to the town of Pleasant Ridge near the Utah border. There's a turquoise house with a wreath of roses on the door. The woman inside is Muriel. She'll tell you what to do next."

One of the behavioral analysts held up a

sign, reminding her to get a fix on his location. "Where will you be? Tell me how I can reach you."

"You need to hurry to make it on time. Bring this phone with you." His tone became more harsh. "Oh yeah, and come alone."

"What if I can't make it? I need to know how to contact you."

"Do as I say. Or this bitch dies."

He ended the call.

She stumbled back a step. Her knees were weak, and she sank into an armchair. If she didn't do as Russell said, he would kill again. She had no choice.

JUST OUTSIDE THE SMALL TOWN of Pleasant Ridge, Dash stared through binoculars at the adobe house painted turquoise. In spite of the wild color, this seemed like a very average household with a small barn in the back and a truck parked at the front door.

He checked his wristwatch. Cara would be here soon. Had he really asked her to marry him? Yeah, that had happened. And he was glad. Now to get her to say yes.

But he couldn't think about that now. It was time to bring Russell down.

They were following his instructions, but

Cara wasn't going in unprotected. Under her jacket, she wore a fitted bulletproof vest. She also had a GPS locating device, a microphone and an earpiece so she could communicate with Dash and the other three agents on dirt bikes.

He spoke into his own headset. "Talk to me, Cara."

"I can see the house. What a god-awful color."

"He's not inside," Dash said. He and the other agents had gotten here earlier and checked it out, hoping that Russell would make a mistake and show himself. No such luck. "Take your time."

He watched as she parked beside the truck, got out of her car and walked up to the door. She knocked once and the door opened. Through the headset, he heard Cara say, "You must be Muriel. I'm Cara."

"You're even prettier than that nice young man said. Come with me."

Through his binoculars, Dash watched as the plump, middle-aged woman led Cara behind the house toward the barn. Through Cara's microphone, he heard the woman— Muriel—chatting about young love and romance and how Russell had paid her one thousand dollars to rent her horse for the evening.

"Horse?" Cara's voice was shaky. "He rented a horse?"

The woman turned and pointed. "Just ride on this trail. It leads into Hovenweep."

"Ride? On the horse? I'm not good at this."

"Your young man seemed to think you were."

"Oh, yeah." Cara's voice quavered between panic and anger. "Everybody looks at me and thinks that because I'm Navajo I can ride. As if all Native Americans are issued a pinto pony and a feather headdress at birth."

"Never mind," Muriel said. "You won't have any problem on Lulu. She's very gentle."

Through the headset, Dash advised Cara that she didn't have to go through with this.

Simultaneously, she answered him and Muriel. "I can handle this."

She was on her way.

Hovenweep National Monument wasn't as famous as Mesa Verde, but Cara had explained to him that many villages had been tucked among these canyons and arroyos. It was a good place to look for pottery shards and arrowheads.

Dash put on his helmet. On his dirt bike, he followed her. The noise from his bike and that of the other two agents might alert Russell, so he kept a distance as he watched her ride slowly along the path. Her horse was a big dappled gray mare that would have been more at home pulling a plow than being ridden.

Through his headset, he heard her grumble, "I can't believe I'm on horseback."

"You're doing great."

"It's not so bad. Lulu is really sweet."

He quickly gave instructions to the other two agents. Stay far back. Make sure they weren't seen. If anyone spotted Russell, they had clearance to open fire. All of these men were sharpshooters.

Carefully, he maneuvered on the rocky hillsides, always keeping her in sight. It was dusk. After dark, it would be more difficult to maintain visual contact.

He heard Cara through the headset. "It's beautiful here. The shadows are a deep purple."

He wanted to tell her that she was the true beauty. As she rode steadily forward on the path, he admired her courage. Never before in his life had he felt such a deep connection to anyone. He would never let her leave him. No matter what it took, he'd make this relationship work. He wanted a home with Cara. A place where they both belonged.

"I'm getting a phone call," she said.

"Hold the phone so I can hear what he says."

He watched as she yanked on the reins and finally got the horse to stop moving. She answered the cell phone.

Russell's instructions were simple. She should turn to the left after she crossed this wide stretch of open land. "You'll see the place," he said. "I marked it with an eagle feather."

Russell had chosen this location well. There was no way for Dash and the other agents to cross this long, flat stretch of sand and sagebrush without being seen. To maintain cover, they needed to go miles out of their way and circle back. They needed time. "Ride slowly, Cara."

"I'll try."

"Remember what I told you," he said. "When you see Russell, give a shout. And get away from him."

"Got it."

While Dash checked in with the other agents, positioning them across the terrain, he watched Cara click her heels against the horse's flank.

Instead of resuming a gentle walk, her mount took off. Cara dug in her heels again and shouted, "Slow down, Lulu."

But the horse went faster. Cara bounced on the saddle. Out of control. Through the microphone, he heard panic in her voice. "I can't get her to stop. Oh my God, I'm going to fall off."

"Pull on the reins."

"I can't." One arm flailed as she tried to keep her balance. "Somebody help me."

He made a split-second decision. There was no way she could handle this horse. She wasn't an experienced rider.

Leaning over the handlebars, he aimed his dirt bike directly across the open land. With all the rocks and ridges, he couldn't go as fast as he wanted, but he was moving. Coming closer to Cara on the runaway steed. They were almost to the other side, near the sandstone ridge.

Less than fifty yards away. Twenty.

He felt a jolt unlike anything he'd ever experienced. He'd been shot.

EVEN THROUGH HER PANIC, Cara heard the gunfire. Her fingers tangled in the horse's mane and yanked. She bounced wildly in the saddle. Slipping to the left, she almost fell before she righted herself.

The horse charged up a rocky hillside, and Cara tilted backward. Was this the place she was supposed to turn? As if she could.

More gunfire. Too much was happening too fast.

Lulu crested the hill and galloped down the opposite side of the ridge. Then, inexplicably, she stopped.

Breathing hard, Cara slid out of the saddle and collapsed in a boneless heap on the ground. Talking to the transmitter hidden in her bra, she said, "Dash? Dash, are you all right?"

Desperately, she needed to hear his voice. But he wouldn't respond.

She reached up and pawed through her hair. Her neat bun had come unfastened. The small plastic piece that had fitted snugly into her ear was gone. Somewhere in her careening ride, she'd lost communication.

Struggling to her feet, she turned. And saw nothing. Not Dash or the other agents. Not Russell. Only the deepening shadows of this desert landscape.

She was alone except for the horse, and there was no way in hell that she'd get back onto that animal.

Moving as quickly as she could, Cara went toward the sandstone rocks, looking for a hiding place.

DASH LAY FLAT ON HIS BACK, staring up. His Kevlar vest had taken the bullet, but the impact had been enough to throw him backward off his dirt bike. Every bone in his body ached. Through the headset, he called her. "Cara, answer me. Where are you?"

Her voice was breathless. "I don't know if you can hear me. I lost my earpiece. I'm on the opposite side of the ridge. Trying to get back."

Other voices came through the headset. Two of the other agents had been shot. Only one was left with transportation.

"Call for backup," Dash instructed.

"I'll come get you," said the one guy with his bike still intact.

"No," Dash said. "He'll pick you off. Stay back."

Good advice. The smart move would be to lie still and let Russell think he was dead. Wait for the backup to arrive. But Cara was up on that ridge. Alone with a madman.

Slowly, Dash turned onto his stomach. He pulled off the helmet that had probably saved his life when he'd hit the ground like a ton of bricks. When he tried to stand, a sharp pain in his left ankle took his breath away. He reached down and felt the swelling. The bone didn't seem broken but this was one hell of a sprain.

He could handle it. He needed to get to Cara.

She huddled inside a narrow crevice. The rough sandstone chafed her hand. If she could get back up to the top of the ridge, she might find Dash and the other agents.

Though she'd heard gunfire, she didn't want to think about what might have happened. She peeked out. The last glimmer of sunlight was fading. Soon it would be dark.

At the top of the ridge there was a break in the rocks. Surely Russell would be watching that natural crossing. She needed to find another route where he'd be less likely to see her.

She stepped away from the crevice.

Russell was there. Waiting. He whispered, "I knew you'd come to me, Cara."

Her gaze darted. Where could she run?

In one hand, he held a rifle. In the other, the stun gun. Remembered pain from his first attack shot through her. "Don't," she said. "Don't use that thing on me again."

"Will you cooperate?"

She had no choice. "Yes."

"Come with me. We'll walk side by side. You deserve to be my equal."

Though she'd lost her earpiece, she hoped the microphone was still working and Dash could hear what Russell was saying. When she saw where they were headed, she tried to give a clue. "It's a cave. A hollow in the rocks."

"It's so much more," he said. "A ceremonial site. With a kiva. And a fire pit."

"Where's the girl you took hostage?"

"You'll see. Soon enough."

She paused to catch her breath. And to think. How could she get out of this? The psychologist had advised her to keep him talking. "I met your father. William Graff."

"Don't talk to me about him."

"Did he hurt you, Russell?"

"He always wanted me to prove myself. To be judged worthy."

She hoped someone else was hearing this because it explained a lot about Russell's need to judge others. "Of course you're worthy. You were always a brilliant student."

They were at the entrance to the shallow

cave—the curved sandstone walls led back about twenty feet. The ground was flat. Arrowheads and pottery shards littered the earth. In the center was a fire pit that had been used many times before. The rock overhead was scorched black.

At the rear of the cave, she saw a young woman with black hair. Bound and gagged. And still very much alive, thank God.

"Don't talk to her." Russell pointed toward the far side of the fire pit. "Sit there."

She lowered herself slowly. Running her hand across the dirt, she found an arrowhead. A weapon.

Russell set aside his rifle and tucked the stun gun into his pocket. He squatted down on the opposite side of the fire pit where twigs and kindling had been laid.

"I smell gas," she said.

"I dumped some on the fire. Kind of got it all over myself."

"Be careful."

"A lot you care." He tossed a match. The flame ignited immediately. He had prepared this fire for some horrible ceremony she didn't even want to imagine.

From across the flames, his gaze met hers. In that instant, he changed. His youth

vanished. In his eyes, she saw an un-
speakable coldness.

"Don't lie," he said. "Don't tell him you
care."

His words made no sense. "Who are you
talking about?"

"You were wrong to leave me," he snarled.

"Russell, I had to—"

"I don't want to hurt you, Cara. I like you."

He had become himself again. A shy
young man with puppy-dog eyes. "Russell?"

"Silence," he thundered. "You deserve to
die."

With a shock, she recognized the voice.
There hadn't been two men at the house
where she'd been held captive. It had been
Russell. *He was two different people.* Jekyll
and Hyde. Her only chance for survival was
to appeal to the kinder Russell.

He stood and paced. Even his posture was
different. His voice was deep and angry. He
growled a string of obscenities.

"Your father hurt you," she said.

"No more talk of him." His leer was
vicious. "Bastard. Bastard."

"You were abused, weren't you? Tell me
about it. I want to understand."

A sob tore from his throat. He knelt and sat
back on his heels. "What's wrong with me?"

"You need help," she said. "Let me help you. There are doctors, psychologists, who can treat you."

"Yeah, sure." Tears creased his cheeks. "I went to the shrinks. They gave me pills that made me weird."

"I'll go with you, Russell. I want to help you."

"You'll leave me." He shrugged. "Everybody leaves me."

Abandonment issues. "I know what that feels like. My father left me, too."

"Believe me, Cara. You don't know what I feel like. Every day it's a fight to keep him quiet."

"Who?"

"It's like there's somebody else inside me. He's the one who hurts those women, then he makes me help him. He wants me to kill you."

He stood. Reaching behind his back, he unsheathed a long, sharp hunting knife.

DASH STRUGGLED DOWN the hillside. Every step was agony, but he couldn't stop. Backup was on the way, but they wouldn't get here soon enough.

He'd listened to Russell. His pathology was clear: a split personality. He'd heard a profiler lecture on this rare condition called dissociative identity disorder, often brought on by physical, emotional or sexual abuse. Russell was a textbook case.

If Cara could keep him talking, Dash might get there in time. He saw the smoke from the cave.

It wasn't far. He could make it.

"PUT DOWN THE KNIFE," Cara said. "You don't have to do this, Russell."

"Yeah, I do." His eyes were sad. "There's only one way to protect you from him. Death."

"No," she said firmly. She had to get control. "Talk to me, Russell. Why are you doing this?"

"I was damaged goods from the very start. My birth parents didn't want me."

"Did they hurt you?"

There was pain. "I don't remember."

There must have been someone good in his life, some good memory she could call upon. "Your mother?"

"Adele. I was never clean enough for her. No matter how many times she took off my clothes and washed me." His lips inched together. "Why couldn't you love me, Cara?"

"I'll help you. I promise."

He raised the knife in his hand. The fire

glittered on the blade. "We both die. Then we'll be together forever."

Before he could take a step, Dash lunged into the cave. He knocked the knife from Russell's hand.

But Russell was quick. Agile. He darted away from Dash. The knife was in his hand again.

Dash positioned himself in front of her. He drew his handgun. "It's over, Russell. You're coming with me."

A peaceful smile crossed his face. He whispered, "Goodbye, Cara."

The blade flashed. Russell had slit his own throat, slashed the carotid artery.

The blood poured out. Thick, red and horrible. Unable to speak, Russell staggered. He toppled forward into the fire. The flames leaped higher as the gas Russell had spilled on his clothing ignited.

Though Dash tried to pull him from the flames and tried to help him, it was over. Russell was dead.

Dash conveyed that information to the rest of the task force. In minutes, they swarmed through the cave. The desolate landscape came alive with men and vehicles and a helicopter with a spotlight, lighting the shadows.

Cara and Dash stepped aside, letting the others do their work. After they'd peeled off their vests and the microphones, they sat side by side on a rock. He wrapped his arm around her shoulders. "You were amazing, Cara."

"I was terrified." After what she'd been through, she couldn't smile. Her features were frozen. "From now on, I'll leave the investigative work to you."

"Even if it's risky?"

"Especially then."

"I'll be careful," he said. "But there's one more risk I need to take. A big one."

"Oh, dear." She sighed. "What is it?"

"I want to settle down, to have a home and become a family. Marry me."

"There's only one logical answer." He was everything she'd ever wanted. And more. "Yes, Dash. We belong together."

* * * * *

*Next month be sure to pick up
COMPROMISED SECURITY,
Cassie Miles's exciting conclusion to her
SAFE HOUSE: MESA VERDE series.*

Turn the page for a sneak preview of
IF I'D NEVER KNOWN YOUR LOVE
by
Georgia Bockoven

From the brand-new series
Harlequin Everlasting Love
Every great love has a story to tell.™

One year, five months and four days missing

There's no way for you to know this, Evan, but I haven't written to you for a few months. Actually, it's been almost a year. I had a hard time picking up a pen once more after we paid the second ransom and then received a letter saying it wasn't enough. I was so sure you were coming home that I took the kids along to Bogotá so they could fly home with you and me, something I swore I'd never do. I've fallen in love with Colombia and the people who've opened their hearts to me. But fear is a constant companion when I'm there. I won't ever expose our children to that kind of danger again.

I'm at a loss over what to do anymore, Evan. I've begged and pleaded and thrown temper tantrums with every official I can corner both here and at home. They've been incredibly tolerant and understanding, but in the end as ineffectual as the rest of us.

I try to imagine what your life is like now, what you do every day, what you're wearing, what you eat. I want to believe that the people who have you are misguided yet kind, that they treat you well. It's how I survive day to day. To think of you being mistreated hurts too much. If I picture you locked away somewhere and suffering, a weight descends on me that makes it almost impossible to get out of bed in the morning.

Your captors surely know you by now. They have to recognize what a good man you are. I imagine you working with their children, telling them that you have children, too, showing them the pictures you carry in your wallet. Can't the men who have you understand how much your children miss you? How can it not matter to them?

How can they keep you away from us

all this time? Over and over, we've done what they asked. Are they oblivious to the depth of their cruelty? What kind of people are they that they don't care?

I used to keep a calendar beside our bed next to the peach rose you picked for me before you left. Every night I marked another day, counting how many you'd been gone. I don't do that any longer. I don't want to be reminded of all the days we'll never get back.

When I can't sleep at night, I tell you about my day. I imagine you hearing me and smiling over the details that make up my life now. I never tell you how defeated I feel at moments or how hard I work to hide it from everyone for fear they will see it as a reason to stop believing you are coming home to us.

And I couldn't tell you about the lump I found in my breast and how difficult it was going through all the tests without you here to lean on. The lump was benign—the process reaching that diagnosis utterly terrifying. I couldn't stop thinking about what would happen to Shelly and Jason if something happened to me.

We need you to come home.

I'm worn down with missing you.

I'm going to read this tomorrow and will probably tear it up or burn it in the fireplace. I don't want you to get the idea I ever doubted what I was doing to free you or thought the work a burden. I would gladly spend the rest of my life at it, even if, in the end, we only had one day together.

You are my life, Evan.

I will love you forever.

* * * * *

Don't miss this deeply moving
Harlequin Everlasting Love story
about a woman's struggle to bring back
her kidnapped husband from Colombia
and her turmoil over whether to let go,
finally, and welcome another man
into her life.
IF I'D NEVER KNOWN YOUR LOVE
by Georgia Bockoven
is available March 27, 2007.

And also look for
THE NIGHT WE MET
by Tara Taylor Quinn,
a story about finding love
when you least expect it.

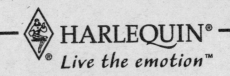

HARLEQUIN®
INTRIGUE®

BREATHTAKING ROMANTIC SUSPENSE

Shared dangers and passions lead to electrifying
romance and heart-stopping suspense!

Every month, you'll meet six new heroes
who are guaranteed to make your spine tingle
and your pulse pound. With them you'll enter
into the exciting world of Harlequin Intrigue—
where your life is on the line
and so is your heart!

THAT'S INTRIGUE—
ROMANTIC SUSPENSE
AT ITS BEST!

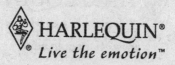

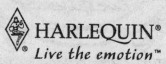

Harlequin® Historical
Historical Romantic Adventure!

Imagine a time of chivalrous knights and unconventional ladies, roguish rakes and impetuous heiresses, rugged cowboys and spirited frontierswomen— these rich and vivid tales will capture your imagination!

Harlequin Historical... they're too good to miss!

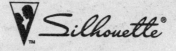